ULTIMATE ENDING

BOOK 7

The Tower of Never There

Check out the full

ULTIMATE ENDING BOOKS

Series:

Treasures of the Forgotten City

The House on Hollow Hill

The Ship at the Edge of Time

Enigma at the Greensboro Zoo

The Secret of the Aurora Hotel

The Strange Physics of the Heidelberg Laboratory

The Tower of Never There

Sabotage in the Sundered Sky

www.UltimateEndingBooks.com

Cover design by Xia Taptara www.xiataptara.com

Internal artwork by Jaime Buckley www.jaimebuckley.com

Enjoyed this book? Please take the time to leave a review on Amazon.

For Chuck Palahniuk, a man who sure knows how to write an ultimate ending.

Welcome to **Ultimate Ending**,
where YOU choose the story!

That's right – everything that happens in this book is a result of decisions YOU make. So choose wisely!

But also be careful. Throughout this book you'll find tricks and traps, trials and tribulations! Most you can avoid with common sense and a logical approach to problem solving. Others will require a little bit of luck. Having a coin handy, or a pair of dice, will make your adventure even more fun. So grab em' if you got em'!

Along the way you'll also find tips, clues, and even items that can help you in your quest. You'll meet people. Pick stuff up. Taking note of these things is often important, so while you're gathering your courage, you might also want to grab yourself a pencil and a sheet of paper.

Keep in mind, there are *many* ways to end the story. Some conclusions are good... some not so good.
Some of them are even great!
But remember:

There is only *ONE*

ULTIMATE ENDING!

THE TOWER OF NEVER THERE

7

Welcome to the Middle of Nowhere!

You are TYLER PAULSEN, rookie hiker, camper, and all-around nice guy. In fact, this happens to be your first camping trip ever. You might even be enjoying yourself... that is if you weren't alone, and so deep in the remote wilderness!

You've spent the better part of the day on this rocky, uncomfortable ridge, staring down into the snowy clearing below. So far, not much has happened. There have been no lights, no sounds... nothing but the constant crackle of your roaring fire. The heat feels good against your back as you crunch down on another bite of granola bar. If only you weren't so thoroughly bored.

The envelopes started arriving more than a year ago. Always blank and with no return address, they came stamped with strange postmarks from all over the world. At first they turned up intermittently and you brushed them off. Then they arrived once a month, until finally, several times each week.

The contents were always the same: a single piece of odd vellum paper. On each, the same set of coordinates, the same date, and two bold words:

Come Alone

Well that date is finally today. And right now? The GPS on your phone tells you you're staring down at the exact spot of those coordinates.

I hope this isn't a joke, you think to yourself. The very thought forces you to look around for maybe the hundredth time. But as you scan the tree-line, it occurs to you that you really have no enemies. And your friends? Well to be honest, none of them are interesting enough to actually pull something like this off.

Besides, watching you sit uneventfully on some cold mountain ridge would be a pretty boring payoff. Especially for such a long con.

No, there has to be a reason for all this. Something important. Something someone went through a tremendous amount of trouble for.

8

Suddenly you feel something. A vibration at first, then a rumble. Your teeth chatter together as the ground begins trembling violently beneath you. The tremors go on for a long moment, driving you from nervous to uncomfortable to outright frightened.

You drop to one knee, reaching for something to steady yourself. Then, just as suddenly as it started, everything comes to an abrupt halt. When you look up again you have the odd sensation that you're still moving, but you soon realize it's only the trees continuing to sway from the aftershock.

An earthquake?

You've never been through one before. You have nothing to compare it to, really. Nothing to say whether–

Your mouth drops open. Down below, the clearing is no longer empty. Impossibly, where there was nothing only moments ago? A gigantic, reaching wall of stone stands before you.

It's tremendous. Ugly. The base of it disappears somewhere in the valley below your campsite. The top is flung high into the mountain mist, lost to the sky.

It's more of a tower, you realize, than a wall. The structure has a definite shape and form to it, but in many places it also doesn't. You find yourself wondering who would design such a thing, and why. But those questions pale in comparison to the even bigger mystery:

How in the world did it get here?

You glance down at your watch. It's nearly dusk. The tower – or whatever it is – stands silhouetted against the dying light. You blink a few times and rub your eyes. Nothing changes. It's still there.

Your foot takes a step forward on its own. The movement is alarming but at the same time it makes you want to laugh. An enormous, hideous-looking tower just erupted into existence seemingly from out of nowhere. And you're actually thinking of checking it out?

As if in answer, the ground rumbles again. *Just an aftershock*, you think. Or maybe something else... *An invitation?*

The sky seems to darken with every passing second. You pull out the latest envelope and stare down at the paper. The writing hasn't changed. It says the same thing as always.

This is the day.

This is the time.

This is the place.

If you're going to explore the tower, you'd better get moving.

9

The hill is steep. Carefully you pick your way downward, crunching through the thin layer of snow while trying to maintain even footing. As you get lower, the tower seems to loom even taller before you. The sheer enormity of it is intimidating.

This is too dangerous, you think to yourself. *I should turn back.* But then you think about all the letters, and all the waiting. All the trouble you took to backpack your way out here, and all the time you spent sitting around, staring at the clearing.

Besides, the tower invited you. Or more accurately, someone *inside* the tower likely did. How could it be dangerous after sending all those letters? That makes sense, right?

Sure it does.

Up ahead, the ground levels out. As you get closer to the structure, you notice a strange mist has formed near the base. It's all grey, and thick, and more than a little foreboding. As you stare into it, it seems to roll and churn with a life of its own.

"Hello?" you call out. Your voice is all but swallowed by the mist. "HELLO?"

Silence answers. You open your mouth to call again, but suddenly feel silly. Maybe if you got a little closer someone would hear you. You're still a long distance away, maybe as much as half a mile. With all the fog it's hard to tell.

I should probably go back and get my things, you think. In your rush down the hillside, you forgot to bring anything with you. No food, no water, not even your utility knife. You feel a little foolish.

As you turn around however, a shudder runs through you. The swirling grey mist has closed in from behind. It envelops you now, blocking your exit. Surrounding you in every direction.

Every direction except straight ahead...

10

You walk slowly, allowing the mist to prod you gently toward the jagged tower. It's getting colder, darker. You miss your campsite, and especially, your fire.

I'm invited, you keep telling yourself. The words are meant to console you, but for some reason you still doubt them. *I was told to come here.* You glance up at the gargantuan stone megalith, looking for answers. It stares impassively down at you, neither menacing nor welcoming.

All around you the air is still, silent. You're standing squarely in the shadow of the tower now. Up ahead, the mist parts in two possible directions. To the left you see a small clearing – an opening in the fog. On your right you see the edge of a forest, preceded by a twisted, gnarled tree. Both ways still lead forward, in the direction you have to go.

Okay, it's time to choose!

If you take the left fork, toward the clearing, *TURN TO PAGE 111*

If you'd rather check out the forest, and the gnarled tree, *HEAD TO PAGE 44*

Or maybe you can still go back for your stuff? To brave the mist and try turning around, *GO TO PAGE 130*

11

You reach up and pluck the magnificent flower. It shimmers through every color of the rainbow as you hand it down to Kara.

"Thank you!" the girl squeals. Carefully she fixes it into her hair, tucking the stem behind one ear.

Una's face is grim. "You were lucky," she says to you. "Look."

The girl points back to the empty vine. For the first time you notice its entire length is covered in wickedly-hooked thorns.

"Whoa."

"Yes," Una agrees. "Whoa."

Kara however, is still beaming. She removes an exquisite jeweled pin from her shirt, leans forward, and then pins it onto your chest.

"Maybe this will help you later," she says, patting the pin. She glances upward. "If you get far enough."

Nice going! Now *TURN TO PAGE 30*

12

COME.

Yeah, you think to yourself. Forget that!

You focus all of your energy on jumping backward. It's like breaking two magnets apart. For a split second it seems impossible, but then you break free all at once and sprawl to the basement floor.

Scrambling to your feet, you turn and run away from the orange thrumming light. When you reach the base of the staircase, you remember something.

You turn around... and walk up the staircase *backwards.*

There's a wild spinning sensation, and suddenly you're back in the garden again. Una and Kara are looking at you expectantly.

Smart move. *TURN TO PAGE 142*

13

Shoving with all your might, you unseat the enormous nightstand from its position beside the bed. It rocks forward...

... but then it tilts back!

The momentum sends the giant piece of furniture crashing downward, directly on top of you! The wind goes out of your lungs as you're pinned to the floor. With your arms and legs trapped at your sides, you can't even move!

The last thing you feel is the heat of the great beast's breath as it bends down and goes face-to-snout with you. As Kavalgyth's lips curl back in a snarl, you're hoping this isn't

---

THE END

14

Beyond the iron gate you enter another area, this one shrouded in darkness. A lit brazier dominates the center of a low-ceilinged room. All around you, a strange purple smoke hangs in the air.

"*The vision chamber,*" YON says dismissively. "*If there were only time, it might actually be of help to you.*"

YON's lights appear muted as he crosses the haze-filled room. You follow him closely, but unlike the being of light and energy, the smoke quickly begins to affect you.

At first, everything seems to slow down. Your head spins, and you're seized by a sense of vertigo. Before you know it you're clutching the wall, breathing deeply, and YON is on the other side of the room.

"*Come,*" he calls to you. His voice is distant. The air tastes sweet in your mouth now, but also sour. Like sugar with lemons...

Uh oh. Roll a single die (or just choose a random number from 1 to 6)

If you roll a 1 or a 2, *GO TO PAGE 94*

If you roll a 3, *HEAD TO PAGE 55*

If you roll a 4 or a 5, *TURN TO PAGE 163*

If you roll a 6, *SKIP DOWN TO PAGE 143*

15

The slat directly beneath you splinters! You make a nimble leap for the next one, but that one breaks too.

This leaves you hanging onto the handholds, dangling from the broken rope bridge as the tremors continue. Maybe once they end, you can swing yourself back up. Maybe there's still a way...

But then you hear it: the dreaded sound of the cables snapping loose from their moorings. The bridge breaks free from the far end of the chasm and you feel yourself drop!

Down, down, down you fall, into the endless violet sky. There doesn't appear to be a bottom (or a top?) – as far as you can see. That is, at least for now.

It's all exceptionally beautiful. But it's also

THE END

16

An elevator? In this place? Yeah... maybe you'd better not.

"Let's take the stairs," you tell Finnegan.

"Ah, a fine choice!"

Without another word Finny leads you through the hall and down another series of corridors. Though you're trying to keep your bearings, you quickly lose track of all the twists and turns.

"Finnegan–"

"Don't worry," he says. "Almost there."

As you round the next corner Finny stops dead in his tracks. There's an enormous concave depression in the hallway. It's almost like someone came along with a giant ice-cream dipper and just scooped out a huge, rounded piece of the wall.

"Ah dang," Finnegan laments. "We missed the stairs." He scratches his head and looks around. "It's not even worth it to look for them."

You're too stunned to even ask any questions. Besides, you're not sure you'd understand the answers anyway. "How do we go up then?"

Finny glances over his shoulder as if looking out for someone again. "Don't worry," he says. "The stairs will be back. Tomorrow, maybe."

"TOMORROW?" You throw your arms up. "I don't have until tomorrow! The tower will blink away by then!"

"Oh," Finny replies. "Alright. Maybe we should try one of the doors, then."

Your eyes go wide. You're approaching the limits of your patience. "But you said *not* to try the doors!"

"Did I?" Finnegan rubs a hand over the stubble of his chin. "That's odd. Some of the doors are actually pretty cool."

"But–"

"Come on," he says. "Let me show you."

Two minutes later you're standing in the middle of the previous hallway. Finnegan points out three different doors. One is oak, one is pine, and the third looks to be made of a soft white material you've never seen before. "These three are good," he says. "Take your pick."

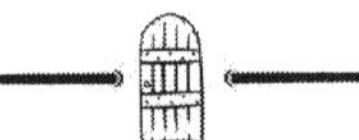

If you choose the oak door, *FLIP DOWN TO PAGE 108*

If you'd rather take the pine door, *HEAD OVER TO PAGE 164*

Or maybe you'd like to open the strange white door? If so, *GO TO PAGE 56*

17

Against every nerve you have, you force the upper half of your body through the opening in the tower wall. Your hands grip both sides of the window's frame like claws as you wait for your eyes to adjust.

"I still can't see anything," you say.

"*Lean further.*"

Your arms are stretched to the limit. "I can't go any furth–"

The kick catches you square in the back, right between the shoulder blades. For a second or two you don't even know what happened. Then you're falling, spinning, tumbling through the sky...

Guess you'll never know what YON was thinking, or why he did what he did. All you can do is hope for the miracle of a soft landing as you hurtle toward

---

THE END

18

The walls shudder. The floor quakes beneath your feet. The unknown voice demands an answer, booming down at you through the chaos.

Master of the tower... master of the tower... the question sings itself to sleep in the back of your mind.

Then, like a thunderclap, a moment of clarity.

...It's me.

Wait... what? *TURN TO PAGE 80*

19

"Nothing in here," you tell YON, hoping it will cause him to step aside. But it doesn't. YON remains firmly planted in the doorway, blocking your exit.

"Come on," you urge him. "Like you said, we've got to keep moving."

YON reaches out and grasps the depressed fountain button. He pulls it toward him with a click, and the door begins sliding closed.

"Wait! What are you–"

The light being says nothing. He flashes bright gold for an instant, then steps back as the door fully closes. Darkness swallows you. You're sealed in the chamber.

"YON!" you scream. "YON!"

More than an hour later you're still screaming, even though you know it's too late. The tower has blinked. You've moved on. There's no chance of ever getting home again.

Maybe YON will let you out of this chamber soon. Maybe not. Either way, you've reached

---

THE END

20

You pass beneath the archway and into a tall, domed chamber. The room is enormous. Moonlight spills in from tall, frosted windows that reach skyward on all sides.

"We made it!" you cry. "We're at the top!"

YON stares back at you without a word. Slowly he nods.

Eight carved pillars are set equidistant from one another around the chamber. They arc overhead to form a colorfully-decorated, pointed ceiling. The artwork above you looks amazing. But it's too far away to see.

"There's no one here," you say. "Where's the–"

YON points. In the middle of the room is a square of four slender pedestals. One is of ebony. One is of ivory. One is carved of soapstone, and the last is formed of pure, glimmering crystal.

The being of light gestures again. "*You must choose*," YON tells you. "*One choice. One trial.*" The voice in your head goes lower, to an almost inaudible level. "*One chance to make things right again.*"

You may have picked up one or more carved figurines during the course of your adventure. If so, now's the time to use them! Choose any one of the following:

If you have the IVORY BALLERINA, you may place it on top of the ivory pedestal and *TURN TO PAGE 180*

If you picked up the EBONY SOLDIER, put that figure on the ebony pedestal and *HEAD TO PAGE 122*

If you own the SOAPSTONE DRAGON, set the creature atop the soapstone pedestal and *GO TO PAGE 41*

If you pocketed the CRYSTAL ANGEL, stand her delicately on the crystal pedestal and *FLIP TO PAGE 72*

Of course it's possible you haven't found any of the figurines yet. If this happens to be the case, *TURN TO PAGE 126*

21

"Peach leaves, huh?"

Kara nods happily. She offers you a bite of peach, but you decline.

For the next minute you crush up the peach leaves and rub them all over you. It smells nice. Sweet. As stealthily as possible, you approach the nest.

"Here goes nothing..."

The hornets swarm! They're all over you! Quickly you turn and run away. Electric shocks shoot up the back of your legs as you're stung three, four, maybe five times.

"Ow ow ow ow!" All of a sudden your voice doesn't work. Kara and Una are standing beside you, looking very sad. When you glance down, your legs are gone! Then your torso, your arms...

"Don't struggle," Una warns. She lets out a long sigh. "It'll only make it slower."

Your body is disappearing! Everything is turning invisible, as if you're dissolving away!

Kara is in tears now. "Don't worry!" she cries apologetically. "You'll come back! I promise!"

Come back? What does she mean by 'come back'?

"The tower won't let you go!"

Finally there's nothing left of your body. Your neck disappears, your head... you experience the most incredible sensation of weightlessness, and then–

You wake up in a field of flowers, sneezing. Everything seems fine. You check your arms, your legs, you even stick out your tongue. Everything's there again!

"You feeling okay?" Una asks.

"I think so," you tell her. "My body tingles a little, but otherwise, yeah."

Kara is smiling again. "The tower remade you," she says. "Now you're a part of it!"

Una's mouth twists. She bumps her sister. "Tell him the rest."

"Oh yeah," Kara says. "But now you can't leave." She frowns. "Like us."

Well, at least now you have all the time in the world to explore the tower. Unfortunately though, this is

---

THE END

22

Thunder crashes. Another bolt of lightning streaks through the sky. You ignore all of these things as you dive for the yellow door...

... and find yourself back inside!

You're in exactly the same room as before. Finnegan stands near the card table, looking back at you strangely.

"Why are you dripping?"

You look down at yourself. Your clothes are soaked. You're standing in a puddle.

"There's no time for swimming," Finny says. "If that's what you were thinking."

"I–"

Finnegan points. A door that wasn't there before stands open in a smooth blank wall.

"Come on," he says, glancing down at his watch. "We've got places to be."

You heard the man! Towel off quickly and *TURN TO PAGE 134*

You yank harder on the doorknob. It still doesn't budge. In the meantime, the pink mist is rising. It fills the room from bottom to top, reaching your waist, your chest, your neck...

"YON..." you cough. "Help me..."

The light-being stares back at you, arms crossed.

"YON!"

"*No*," he says finally. "*I will not help*."

Not cool YON, not cool! Things are looking bleak, but you still have a chance...

Roll a single die (or just pick a random number from 1 to 6)

If the number is a 1 or a 6, *TURN TO PAGE 165*

If the number is a 2, 3, 4, or 5, *HEAD OVER TO PAGE 103*

24

The snow globe must do *something*, you think to yourself. Quickly you pull it out and shake it.

Inside the crystal globe, snow falls on the garden scene. It's all very tranquil. But the dancer doesn't seem to notice. She keeps on coming, spinning faster and faster, heading directly toward you...

The globe isn't having any effect. You'll have to choose again!

There's not a lot of time! Pick something else:

If you have the Lotus Blossom, try giving it to her *ON PAGE 121*

If you have the Jeweled Pin you can try that *BY FLIPPING TO PAGE 173*

If you have the Bone Horn, blow it quickly *OVER ON PAGE 67*

If you have none of these items, *TURN TO PAGE 137*

25

"The answer," you say, "is twenty-five."

The sphinx remains motionless, but its grin widens ever so slightly. "*How so?*"

"Well, you have one-hundred *more* than your wife," you explain. "So if your wife has twenty-five, one-hundred more than that would give you one twenty-five." You let out a long, deep breath. "Add those together and you get one-fifty."

YON twinkles. The sphinx nods in approval.

"*That is correct.*"

Shifting to one side, the sphinx moves to allow you full access to the exit arch. YON passes beneath it first. On your way through however, the sphinx leans in close and whispers to you:

"*Even the ugliest of beasts can appreciate great beauty,*" the creature hints.

You wonder what that means. Maybe it's important.

Nodding politely, you keep going.

Very nice work there! Now *FLIP BACK TO PAGE 20*

26

You pull at the tentacles. You shove at them. But it's no use! No matter what you do, your hands slide right through them!

"I can't get hold of them!" you shout to Kara and Una. But they have their own problems. Kara is already up to her waist in the mud. Una, even further.

"Stop moving!" cries Kara. "Don't do anything at all!"

Since your struggle only seems to make things worse, you heed her advice. You will yourself to stop moving. It's not an easy task, especially with the mud tentacles sliding uncomfortably along your body.

But it works.

"She's right!" you shout to Una. "Don't move!"

By remaining utterly still, the tentacles actually lose interest. They release their hold on you and sink slowly back into the mud.

"How'd you know to do that?" you ask Kara.

She looks sheepish. "I, uh... I might've run into these things once or twice."

"Once or *twice?*" Una crows. Her green eyes flash as she wrings mud from her hair. "And you led us through here *anyway?*"

"Well..."

The sisters, you realize, could argue all day. You don't have all day. You don't even have an hour. "At least we're across," you say diplomatically. "So could we please keep going?"

Una nods, Kara smiles, and together you all slog out of the pond. At the water's edge, the blue-eyed twin plucks a pair of beautiful lotus blossoms. She inhales deeply from one and holds the other one out to you.

"One for me," Kara says, "and one for you." As you take it, she turns her nose up at her sister. "None for you."

Jump back on the path again *OVER ON PAGE 133*

27

"Hang on," you tell your friend. "I'm gonna climb it." Finnegan winces visibly but says nothing.

Before you lose your nerve, you step on the statue's base and pull yourself up. The surface is smooth but not slippery. It also feels warm beneath your touch. You don't have to go far to read the inscription, which you repeat out loud:

Ice can reach

Where angels soar

Frosted wings

Drawn to the floor

"Well it sure doesn't look like an angel," Finnegan says. He cocks his head and tries looking at the statue from different angles.

You shimmy down and jump back to the floor. "It doesn't feel like one either." Hesitantly you look down at your palms. The skin isn't turning green or peeling away. It looks like you might be safe after all.

"How would you even know what an angel feels like?" Finny asks.

You ignore the question. "Alright," you tell him. "I'm ready now."

Follow Finnegan out of the creepy statue room by *TURNING TO PAGE 66*

28

The hallway ends in an old, dilapidated chamber. Strange floral wallpaper peels from broken plaster walls, curling downward in tatters. There are piles of it all over the floor, shredded by time.

"I don't see any exits," you say. "Should we go back?"

YON shakes his head. "*It is too late to go back.*" He points to where four stone blocks protrude slightly from the wall beside you. Each is etched with a different symbol.

"These look like buttons," you say.

YON nods.

"Okay fine. So which do I press?"

"*I cannot answer that,*" he says. "*However, the answer is all around you.*"

You glance around. Once, twice, then three times. "There's nothing here!" you cry in frustration. "Nothing but a bunch of shredded wallpaper."

Once again the light-being nods. Only this time you get the distinct impression he might be smirking.

29

You reach down and pick up a scrap of wallpaper. Focusing on it intently, you examine the odd floral pattern...

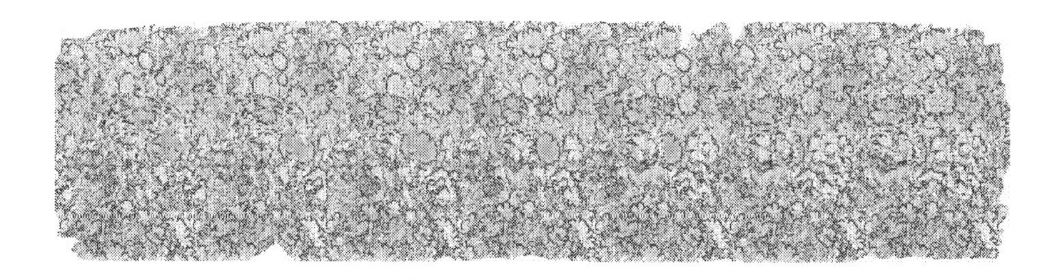

[This image is a **Stereogram**. If you stare at a point *beyond* the image, and slowly unfocus/cross your eyes, a distinct 3D shape should emerge.]

[The best advice would be to relax your eyes. If you can manage to get your vision off focus, at some point you will be able to see the hidden image.]

[Some people can see Stereograms easily. Others can't see them at all. Hopefully you're not one of the latter!]

If you can see the Stereogram, you *know* which button to press.
Otherwise, you'll just have to guess:

To press the button with the SEASHELL on it, *TURN TO PAGE 38*
To press the button with the GRYPHON SHIELD on it, *GO TO PAGE 49*
To press the button with the FOUNTAIN on it, *HEAD TO PAGE 120*
To press the button with the CROSSED SWORDS on it, *FLIP TO PAGE 76*

30

The stone path continues through the garden, this time past a field of vibrant blue-green grass. A small animal scurries by. The whistle of a bird is answered by several more. Abruptly, something occurs to you.

"Where's all the light coming from?"

You hadn't thought about it before, but by now it should be almost dusk. Yet the inside of the tower is lit from above, as if under constant sunshine.

"From above?" Kara shrugs. Una gives her a look.

You glance up again, toward a ceiling that must be ten stories overhead. There's no central source of illumination. Somehow light seems... everywhere.

The path splits again, left and right. Nestled between the fork is a large, moss-covered boulder. There's a message carved into it, partially covered with undergrowth. You step off the path to brush it clean.

Back to Move Forward, Down to Go Up

The Mirror of Reason, Fills Chaos's Cup

"What does *that* mean?" you ask. The sisters only stare back at you. "And who wrote it?"

Kara looks thoughtful. "I don't know, Tyler. Who do *you* think wrote it?"

You laugh. "Like I should know! You two are the ones that live here."

"Not always," says Una. She bites her lip and looks down. Kara nods, and you feel suddenly terrible.

"Oh. Sorry."

"Don't be," Kara smiles. "This place isn't all that bad."

You find yourself wondering how the twins got there, and where they came from. Whether or not they'll be able to leave. A million questions spring to mind, but you don't ask them.

"Come on," Una tells you. "You should probably hurry."

To take the LEFT path, *FLIP TO PAGE 166*
Or you can choose the RIGHT path, *OVER ON PAGE 105*

31

You pull out the carved bone horn and blow it as hard as you can... right into the angel's face!

Uh oh!

The angel screams. LOUDLY. Half from fright, half out of rage, it screams right back at you with the fury of... well... a screaming, scornful angel.

Have you ever heard an angel scream? The sound is like nails being dragged on a chalkboard... a thousand times over. In other words, it *physically* hurts.

The noise drives a chill through your body. A spike through your soul. The horn is an afterthought as you sink to your knees, head in your hands, fighting just to keep everything from going black...

You wake up cold and alone. Light shines in through the windows of the upper tower chamber. It's day!

The tower has blinked. The landscape outside is something you don't even recognize.

You missed your shot.

Sorry, but this is

THE END

32

You pull out the lotus blossom Kara gave you in the indoor garden. Maybe it will help. Maybe it will–

Whoosh!

The soldier's latest attack narrowly misses you! You drop the flower and back up. There's nothing to do but run...

"YON!" you scream. But there's no answer. With the warrior hot on your heels, you flee into the darkness. Shadows rush past you. Objects... people... *are those trees?*

WHAM!

You awaken, shivering in the darkness. The chamber is empty. No one is around.

Rubbing your head, you crawl to one of the windows. The snow-covered mountains are gone. In their place is nothing but a flat horizon. A vast, reaching desert that stretches in every direction...

The tower!

You look up. Three differently-sized moons dominate the sky. One of them is blood red. It's the strangest thing you've ever seen, and in the last hour or so, you've seen some pretty strange things!

It blinked...

Wherever you are now, it's no longer here. Or there. It's someplace else. Which of course makes this

---

THE END

33

The path is old, the stones worn with time. They're set into earth that's moist and mossy, even though the rest of the surrounding area is dry as a bone.

The further you continue down the path, the more it seems out of place. Like the ground the path is set upon just doesn't belong. Many of the later stones are upended. They stick up at odd angles from the ground, causing you to step around them.

Slowly, insidiously, the mist continues to creep in. It closes in from behind at first, then starts pressing in on the path from both sides. You feel trapped. Claustrophobic. You start doubting yourself, wondering if you made the right choice.

Just then, it begins to rain. Large, heavy droplets of icy water pelt down on you from above. The water gets in your eyes... and it stings! It burns wherever it touches your skin too, almost like...

Acid!

That old bridge is looking better and better all of a sudden. Maybe you can still make it back. If you want to turn around and try, *RUN TO PAGE 159*

On the other hand, you've already come pretty far. The tower can't be that much further... can it? To keep forging ahead, *SPEED DOWN TO PAGE 65*

34

There isn't time to wait! Adroitly, you swing the branch back with one arm. But just as nimbly, Kara plucks it from your hand!

The snake keeps coming. You move to kick it... but you miss by a mile. Completely off balance, you fall to the hard cobbles of the stone path. Pain rockets along your shoulder.

"Stop it!" Kara cries. "Stop it right now!"

The serpent finally reaches the girls. Una stands frozen in horror. But Kara kneels and extends her hand... and the snake crawls right up her arm! It coils gently around her neck and over her shoulder before it finally stops, happily flicking its tongue in and out.

Kara gives you and her sister a dirty look. "This is my *friend*," she says in wounded tones. "He wouldn't harm a soul." Turning her head, she nuzzles the snake nose to nose. "You're lucky you didn't hurt him!"

You and Una exchange the same look of dismay. Red-faced, you brush yourself off and return to your feet.

"I'm sorry," you tell Kara. "I really am. I didn't know."

Though she still looks unhappy, her expression softens. "Fine," she says. "Apology accepted." Gingerly Kara extracts the snake from her shoulders and places it in the grass. She pats it once on the head and it slithers away.

"Let's go."

Better do what she says. *HEAD TO PAGE 148*

35

You look up at the ceiling, then down at the pole. "No way I'm poking around up there," you tell Finnegan.

"Please?" Finny asks.

"No." You try handing it back to him. "I don't know what's up there. And besides, we have to keep–"

Before you can react, Finnegan closes his hand over your own and forces you to choose!

Roll a single die. (Or just pick a random number from 1 to 6)

If you rolled a 1 or 2, *TURN TO PAGE 45*

If you rolled a 3 or 4, *TURN TO PAGE 174*

If you rolled a 5 or 6, *TURN TO PAGE 140*

36

Again the minotaur comes at you! But this time you're not so lucky. You zig when you should've zagged, and you end up stepping right *into* the creature's attack.

WHAM!

You wake up groggy, in total darkness. It feels like someone opened the top of your head and poured a bag of sand in there! Tentatively you reach up... and find a bump the size of an orange on the back of your skull.

Slowly you crawl your way across the cold, stone floor. You're in a cell. Thick steel bars keep you trapped in one corner of the room, with no hope of escape.

A quick check of your pockets shows all your things are gone. You have no idea how much time has passed. But it doesn't matter.

You're stuck in the tower now, and that means you've reached

THE END

You gaze out over the pond. It looks quiet and still. The water is smooth as glass. "It's only knee-deep?" you ask Kara.

"Yes."

"You're sure?"

"Uh huh." She nods vigorously.

"Alright, fine then," you say. "If it'll save us some time let's just wade through."

Leading the way this time, the three of you start across the water. Aside from the soft bottom sucking against your boots, it's pretty easy going. You're a quarter of the way across, then halfway. In fact you're almost to the opposite edge, when something shifts beneath you.

"What was–"

Long finger-like appendages shoot up from the water, surrounding you in every direction. They move like snakes, wrapping themselves around your legs as they begin pulling you downward!

"Oh..." Kara has one finger in her mouth.

"Oh what!" you cry out.

"I forgot about these," she tells you. "They're mud tentacles."

"MUD TENTACLES!" you shout. "How could you forget about–"

Your sentence is cut off as one of the brown tendrils wraps itself over your mouth. You grab it... and your hand squishes right through the soft, clay-like substance. But at least now you can breathe!

There's no time to lose! Roll two dice (or just pick a random number from 2 to 12)

If the number comes up a 1, 2, 6, 8, or 11, *GO TO PAGE 84*

If the number is a 3, 4, 5, 7, 9, 10, or 12, *TURN TO PAGE 26*

38

The seashell button look innocuous. With no time to waste, you reach out and press it.

There's a hollow *click* from somewhere behind the wall. You wait, cringing, as long seconds tick by. The seconds drag into a minute. Nothing happens.

Finally you glance back at YON. Did he just shrug? He's pointing to the panel of buttons again.

Guess that one's broken. Give it another shot:

To try the button with the GRYPHON SHIELD on it, *GO TO PAGE 49*

To try the button with the FOUNTAIN on it, *HEAD TO PAGE 120*

To try the button with the CROSSED SWORDS on it, *FLIP TO PAGE 76*

39

The unblemished diamond is on the other side of the mirror. You need to get to it...

There's a block of broken stone at your feet, and an idea comes to mind. You don't over-think it. With one arm you scoop up the brick, rear back, and smash the mirror!

The Tyler on the other side of the glass doesn't even flinch. For a brief moment he looks overwhelmingly sad, and then his image is lost in a maelstrom of glittering, shimmering glass.

Your vision blurs as jagged shards rain down all around you. Then, everything goes wonky. The floor twists beneath you, and seems to dissolve. The walls of the tower waver as if made out of crepe paper. You look up and the stars are gone – even the skylight too! Somehow you're staring up into a broad expanse of violet sky that stretches from horizon to horizon. A chill in the air tells you a steady breeze just picked up.

You look down...

You're back at your campsite! It's not even dark yet, it's still just before dusk. You're sitting on a rock, staring down from a ridge. From the heat on your back you can tell that your fire is still roaring.

Your gaze is fixed on the clearing below. Like you're looking for something...

What was it?

Or maybe waiting on something.

Waiting on what?

Unconsciously you bring your hand up to your mouth. You're holding a half-eaten granola bar. You take another bite. Man, you're hungry! Thirsty too. Not to mention a little tired.

The clearing. What's the deal with–

Suddenly you feel something. A rumble at first, then a steady vibration. The ground is trembling! Maybe it's an earthquake...

Well, it certainly looks like you have an adventure ahead of you! Good luck with that.

For this time around however, we're calling it

THE END

40

There's not a lot of time, and that staircase isn't going to climb itself. Better get started.

You place one foot on the first step. It seems solid. If you can just concentrate on your footing, and somehow not look down? Everything will be fine. You hope...

Step by careful step you ascend the staircase. But with each step, things get inexplicably darker. You start to feel weird; your head is buzzing and your body doesn't feel like it's going forward. You're off balance. And that's when you realize you're walking *backwards.*

Finally you stop and look up from your feet. You're standing in the basement! Inky blackness stretches in every direction except for one. Straight ahead, you can make out what's best described as a pulsating orange glow.

Suddenly you're walking toward it. Your feet have apparently taken on a mind of their own. The orange glow gets brighter, the pulses increasing in frequency, and now, in volume too.

THRUM! THRUM! THRUM!

You can feel the light as well as see it. It's like a heartbeat. A vibration in the air. You're still walking forward, directly into the light, only now it's becoming so bright it's actually hurting your eyes.

It takes all of your willpower to stop. As your feet come together you still feel the draw of the light. The pull of something *within* the light, urging you on.

COME.

Your foot twitches. One of your knees bends.

COME.

Again you will yourself to stop. The pulling sensation is more powerful than ever. It's getting difficult and almost painful to resist. Letting yourself go would be so much easier...

Maybe this is where I'm supposed to be. You think back to the letters, all of which said 'come alone'. *Maybe this is who invited me here...*

Your body jerks. You're being pulled forward again. In a few more seconds, you'll be too close to do anything about it. You're not sure how you know this, but you do.

Wanna see what's inside the orange light? Of course you do! End the curiosity *OVER ON PAGE 115*

Wait, what? Where am I? Break on out of here *BY TURNING TO PAGE 12*

41

You pull out the carved stone dragon Finnegan stole from the minotaur. It's made from exactly the same material as the soapstone pedestal.

Shrugging, you step forward and place the figurine on top of it.

The figure begins to move. It writhes, curls... then grows! Soon it engulfs the middle of the room, stretching wide, leathery wings as it unfurls to its full, terrifying length.

"Uhhh... YON?"

But your friend the light-being is no longer there. In fact, the walls and windows of the chamber are gone as well. There's dirt beneath your feet. Shimmering waves of grass brush past your ankles. And above, high overhead, a star-filled sky...

The dragon stretches. It sniffs the air a few times, then turns in your direction. Its piercing yellow eyes drill into your own.

The creature roars! Slowly, deliberately, it cranes its neck downward in your direction...

Ummm... maybe you'd better do something? And quick!

If you have the Lotus Blossom you can offer it to the dragon *ON PAGE 177*

If you have the Jeweled Pin, try giving that to the dragon *ON PAGE 81*

If you have the Bone Horn, you can try blowing it *OVER ON PAGE 161*

If you have the Snow Globe, try shaking it vigorously and *HEAD TO PAGE 128*

Oh, and if you happened to pet the Saspernink? Ignore all the above choices and flip immediately *OVER TO PAGE 136*

If you obtained or accomplished none of these things, *TURN TO PAGE 68*

42

The minotaur is rushing at you with surprising speed. There's no time to do anything but get out of the way!

Leaping to one side, you find yourself next to one of the bedroom night tables. It's big enough to be an armoire.

"Tyler!"

Finnegan is up on the bed now. He points to the over-sized nightstand and makes a shoving motion. There's no time to even acknowledge him. You lower your shoulder into the thing and push...

Hurry! Roll two dice! (Or just pick a random number from 2 to 12)

If you roll a 2 or a 12, *TURN TO PAGE 13*

If you roll a 3, 4, 10, or 11, *FLIP TO PAGE 147*

If you roll a 5, 6, 7, 8, or 9, *HEAD DOWN TO PAGE 158*

43

Reaching into your pocket, you draw out the crystal snow globe. As the angel plummets in your direction, you shake it...

Suddenly the room fills with snow!

A cold wind swirls through the chamber, spinning out in tornado-like fashion. The weather exactly mimics the small blizzard going on within the snow globe. Glimmering crystals begin to appear, clinging to every surface of the room. The walls, the dome... icicles form, and everything soon sparkles with frost.

Up above, the angel shrieks! Snow and ice have coated its wings, dragging it downward and toward the floor. You step back as she flutters in panic, doing her best not to crash. Eventually she settles to the ground not far from where you're standing.

The angel delivers you a mischievous smirk. She looks disappointed! But oddly enough, also respectful. She bows her head once in slow acknowledgment. Then, right before your very eyes, she fades away!

"*That was... impressive.*"

YON is standing beside you again. It makes you wonder where he was this whole time!

"*There.*"

Your friend points. A rounded section of the floor is slowly rising in the center of the chamber. Without a second thought you jump on.

"*Farewell,*" YON tells you mentally. But when you look back for him again, he's gone.

The floor continues to rise. You're being lifted toward the upper dome.

To the highest point in the tower...

Awesome job! Now enjoy the ride before *TURNING TO PAGE 100*

44

You make your way in the direction of the wood, being careful not to wander too close to the strange grey mist. Oddly the snow ends, and a strong, earthy smell fills your nostrils. Like smoldering mulch, or even decay.

An immense gnarled tree presides over the entrance to the forest. Its twisted roots dig in and out of the soft ground, like the diving coils of some legendary sea serpent. Your eyes are following the curve of branch and trunk when you notice something glimmering in a pile of dead brush. Reaching down, you pick it up.

It's a crystal figurine, beautifully carved into the likeness of an angel. It appears to be mid-flight, its wings both delicate and exquisitely detailed.

Without wondering how it got there, you pocket the treasure and move on. The path leading into the forest is winding and narrow, but thankfully free of the weird, swirling fog.

You're a few meters down the path when a noise stops you. Somewhere in the canopy overhead, you hear a rustling sound in the leaves. The noise is accompanied by shifting shadows. As you strain to peer into the darkness, a terrifying shriek sends a shiver of ice down your spine.

The creature looks like a vulture, or maybe a bat. Possibly even a little of both. Erupting from the canopy before soaring toward you, it extends talons that end in sharp, curved claws...

How fast can you move? Flip two coins, one right after the other.

If both coins come up HEADS, *TURN TO PAGE 69*

If either (or both) come up TAILS, *HEAD DOWN TO PAGE 146*

45

Finnegan looks at you pleadingly. He reminds you of a begging dog.

"Fine," you say, humoring him. "One poke."

Grabbing the pole, you insert it into the nearest hole. It goes in for about a foot, then encounters soft resistance.

"Nothing there," you say. "It's just a hole."

But Finny isn't convinced. "Come on," he says. "You didn't even poke it!"

Pulling your arm back, you jab upward. The pole pierces something pliable, but then you feel it go through.

A torrent of liquid rushes forth from the hole, showering you with smelly water. It gets on your arms, your chest, your clothes... It's vile and disgusting.

Finnegan makes a face. "Awww, gross."

"Yeah," you say snapping the pole over your knee. "Gross."

Jeeze! Why do you even listen to this guy? *HEAD ON DOWN TO PAGE 66*

46

You reach for the card with the shadowy figure on it. Before your fingers even touch the surface you notice how cold it is.

"It's like a block of ice," you tell Finnegan. But your friend doesn't answer. His face is serious, his look grim. You touch the card...

Everything disappears.

All of a sudden you're outdoors again! A cold, steady rain streams down from the sky. Lightning flashes, silhouetting something dark and ominous just beside you. That something is also gigantic...

You're at the base of the tower!

"Finnegan!"

You scream your friend's name into the rain. There's no response. You're about to yell again when a bolt of lightning rips the ground only a few yards away! The sheer power of the impact drives you right to your knees.

"Finny..." you cough. The word catches in your throat. The air is charged with electricity – it feels thick and hostile and even alive. You're kneeling now in rivulets of slush and frozen mud. It takes every effort just to lift your head back into the rain.

When you do, you see two distinct glowing doorways. One is yellow, one is blue. They're not far off.

Thunders roars as you stumble forward in that direction. You don't care where either of the doors go, as long as that place isn't *here.*

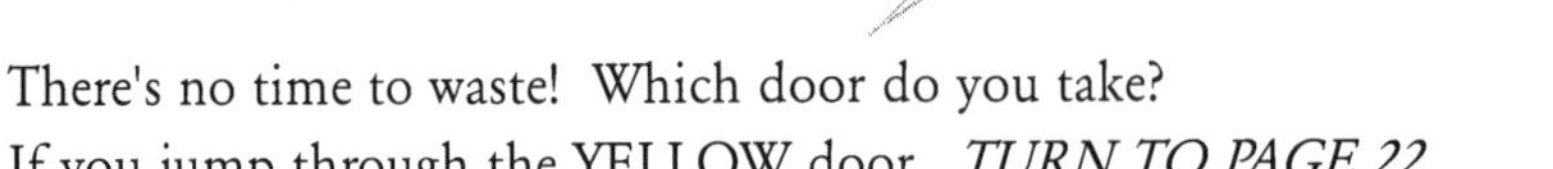

There's no time to waste! Which door do you take?

If you jump through the YELLOW door, *TURN TO PAGE 22*

If you stumble through the BLUE door instead, *GO TO PAGE 172*

47

The booming noise down the path makes you nervous. And for some reason, your gut feeling tells you the cave is the way to go.

Pulling out your phone, you activate the flashlight feature. It works wonderfully in the darkness, providing enough light to illuminate the entire inside of the cave. Tentatively you step inside.

You walk for a while, avoiding side passages and down-slopes while sticking to the main cavern. The cave is clean and wide and cuts more or less straight through the small hillside. And thankfully, it's also empty.

Eventually however, the main cavern ends. As you scan the walls with your flashlight the chattering sound comes back... followed by a high-pitched screeching noise from just overhead. Reluctantly you shine the flashlight upward...

Bats!

They're everywhere! Thousands of them cover the ceiling in a living wave, and now they're starting to stir!

A couple of the creatures drop from the roof of the cave, then a few more. Soon there are dozens of them, fluttering around you in jerky, broken circles. They dip low, obscuring your vision. Not wanting to stick around, you break into a run!

Two passages break from the main cavern, one narrow and one wide. No time to waste... you'd better pick one fast!

To take the wide passage that slopes downward, *TURN TO PAGE 149*

To take the narrow passage that slopes upward, *HEAD ON OVER TO PAGE 74*

48

Finnegan has led you a long way. And so far, he hasn't steered you wrong.

On a whim – and before you lose your nerve – you grab hold of him without thinking and jump!

Of course, you fall. You expected that. As you tumble through the air you surrender to gravity, allowing it to pull you down, down, down through the darkness. You're just about second-guessing your decision when all of a sudden...

SQUISH!

Your body slams through something soft and spongy and very, very weird. As your senses return you find yourself covered in chunky goo. You're lying flat on your back, staring up into the ribbed underbelly of a giant mushroom cap!

"Ohhh..." Finny groans from beside you. "Man, that was a lot further than I thought it was!"

You rise slowly and find yourself in a different world. Or at least, it looks that way. Mushrooms and toadstools tower over you like buildings. One of them has a Tyler-sized hole in it from where you fell through!

"Where are we?" you ask, afraid of the answer. You're torn between utter disbelief and being grateful just to be alive.

"The fungi garden," Finnegan answers. He thumps the side of a giant toadstool. "Or at least, that what I've always called it."

The ground beneath you is a spongy mass of soft green moss. It's difficult to walk.

"Kavalgyth planted them," Finny adds. "I think he eats them."

"Kavalg–"

"Never mind that," your friend tells you. He glances over his shoulder for the umpteenth time. "Come. We have to hurry."

Together you run across the springy damp earth, making your way toward a large exit. "By the way, you're crazy!" Finnegan calls back. "And I mean that in the best possible way."

Follow Finnegan out of mushroom-land by *TURNING TO PAGE 112*

49

You place your hand over the gryphon button and push. There's the distinct grinding of stone on stone, and a door opens in the wall beside you.

When you poke your head through, you see nothing but a plain hallway.

"Is this–"

YON answers by ushering you through. The door grinds noisily closed behind you.

Together you walk, with YON once more allowing you to take the lead. After a short while the corridor ends in a 'Y'-shaped intersection.

Looks like you're in charge!

To take the LEFT fork, *TURN TO PAGE 113*

To take the RIGHT fork, *FLIP DOWN TO PAGE 179*

50

"This one isn't even a challenge," you say confidently. "The answer is fifty."

The sphinx cocks its head. "*Why?*"

"Because together the man and his wife have one-hundred and fifty gold," you say. "You have one-hundred more than her, so she has fifty. fifty plus one-hundred equals one-fifty."

You start toward the archway, but the sphinx shifts its weight to block you.

"*That is not the answer.*"

You blink. "Of course it is."

"*I assure you it is not,*" the Sphinx says firmly. "*You have one hundred* more *than her. So if she has fifty, that would give you one-hundred fifty. Together, that would make two-hundred.*"

Your heart sinks. The sphinx is right.

"Uhhh, okay," you say hesitantly. Something about the look in the sphinx's eye causes you to let out a nervous chuckle. "You win this round. You got me!"

"*Yes,*" YON says sadly. "*He does.*"

You feel a bump. When you look down, there's a glowing red chain clamped around your ankle. The other end of the magical chain disappears somewhere beneath the sphinx's great bulk.

"Ummm," you groan apprehensively, "got any *other* riddles? Wanna try again?"

"*Yes,*" replies the sphinx. "*Eventually.*"

YON goes on to explain how the sphinx has bound you to servitude for a period of one year. Which is nothing, he adds, when you consider he himself has been here for almost a full millennium.

Wow, not good! But look on the bright side: at least you'll have plenty of time to bone up on your riddle-answering skills.

See you next year! Until then, this is

THE END

51

With no time to waste, you pull out the carved bone horn. You've never tried something like this before. You put it to your lips, take a deep breath, and...

A sound blares forth, mournful and low. It echoes through the darkness, shattering the stillness of the air.

The soldier stops advancing. He cocks one ear to the sky.

He turns away from you!

You lower the horn warily. As if answering some unseen call, the warrior pivots on one heel and stomps off in another direction.

The darkness fades. The ground is once again smooth beneath your feet. You're back in the chamber!

YON is there too. He's pointing. In the center of the room, a platform has begun slowly rising from the floor.

You jump on...

Fantastic! Ride the platform up, up, up into the next area *OVER ON PAGE 100*

52

There's something about YON you're not entirely comfortable with. Also, leaning dangerously far out an open window isn't high on your list of priorities.

"Forget it," you tell the light-being. "Is it your job to get me to the top of the tower?"

YON flashes orange for a moment. It's something you construe as annoyance, maybe even anger. His posture, however, is of compliance.

"Good. Then lead the way."

The golden figure hesitates as if contemplating. When he finally does move, it's in the direction of another staircase.

You let out a long sigh. "More steps?"

YON nods.

"This is getting old."

You have good instincts, especially when it comes to self-preservation. Now *TURN TO PAGE 170*

The stone path winds itself through the amazing indoor garden. Trees sprout on both sides, tall, green and healthy. Flowers are planted everywhere you look. Some are so strange and exotic you don't ever remember seeing them before.

You follow Una and Kara, and it's not easy to keep up. The girls dance along the path as if they'd lived here their whole lives, a thought which has you wondering...

Abruptly they stop. The path splits in a perfect 'Y' shape. On the left fork, a wooden sign is embedded into the ground. Individual letters have been tacked into the sign, but some of them have fallen to the ground.

"Hmm..." Una says, placing a finger on her chin. "I don't remember *that* being there."

You reach down pick up three fallen letters. You find a '**G**', a '**D**', and an '**E**'.

Shuffling the letters back and forth in your hands, you glance up. "I think I know what the sign says," you say. "In fact–"

"Wait," Kara jumps in. "Here, I found another letter." She hands you another '**E**'.

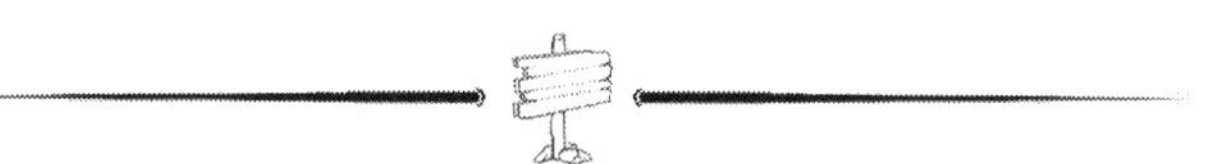

Still think you know what the sign says?

If you think it spells '**DANGER**', *GO TO PAGE 141*

If you think the sign spells something else, *GO TO PAGE 95*

54

The floor shifts. The tower trembles. You look up through the skylight and into the cold, bright stars.

"YON," you say firmly. "The master of the tower is YON."

There's a pause. A moment of nothing. Then the booming voice speaks again in reply:

YON HAS BEEN HERE LONGER THAN ALL. HE HAS LIVED MANY LIFETIMES. HE HAS GARNERED GREAT POWER.

The walls shake. Dust rains down all around you.

BUT NO. YON IS NOT THE MASTER.

You're about to open your mouth in protest when the voice speaks once more:

CHOOSE AGAIN.

Whew! Another chance! Better make it count.

If you *know* who the master of the tower is, use the chart below to add up all the letters in that word. When you have the total you can *GO TO THAT PAGE*

A = 1	F = 6	K = 11	P = 16	U = 21	Z = 26
B = 2	G = 7	L = 12	Q = 17	V = 22	Example:
C = 3	H = 8	M = 13	R = 18	W = 23	ANNA =
D = 4	I = 9	N = 14	S = 19	X = 24	1+14+14+1
E = 5	J = 10	O = 15	T = 20	Y = 25	= 30

If you still don't know who the master is, *TURN TO PAGE 60*

55

You're trying to get to YON but you just can't. Every joint in your body seems locked up. Your feet feel like they weigh a thousand pounds each.

Sliding along the wall, you drop to one knee. The mist parts, and you can see the silhouette of a woman in the shadows.

She's dancing. Swinging her arms overhead as she prances gracefully around the room. You squint, trying to make her out, but there are no features. The mist is too thick. She's moving too fast.

"YON!" you try to call out. Your voice is swallowed, lost like a sigh in a thunderstorm. The dancer spins faster now, always in circles. At each turn you notice something flashing at you through the purple smoke.

Gems? Jewels?

The dancer stops, but the room is still whirling. Or maybe it's your head that's spinning. You blink hard, trying to clear your vision, when you sense motion again.

Someone approaches. Or something...

What is it? Find out *OVER ON PAGE 163*

56

You point at the strange door. Before you can even open your mouth, Finny grabs the handle.

"Ah," he says happily. "I was hoping you'd pick that one!" He opens the door and ushers you in.

The chamber is an elaborate bedroom. It's also very large. The ceiling is twice normal height, and the over-sized furniture is carved into beautiful, nature-inspired designs. A fireplace roars in the opposite wall, blanketing the room in a warm, inviting glow.

"Good!" Finnegan says. "He's not here." Immediately your friend begins rifling through the room. He looks under the massive bed then starts tearing open dresser drawers.

"Whose room is this?"

"Kavalgyth's."

"Should we be here?" you ask nervously.

"Uhhh... probably not for long," Finny replies. "So help me look?"

You have a very bad feeling about this. "What are we looking for?"

Finnegan grunts as he moves a large piece of furniture. He looks confused for a moment. "I'll know it when I see it."

Know it when you see it? You clap both hands to the sides of your head in exasperation. "Well can you give me a hint?"

CRASH!

Suddenly the door to the room flies open. It cracks against the opposite wall and shatters into a dozen wicked-looking pieces.

"Uh oh," Finny says.

A creature stands in the doorway. It has the body of a large, well-muscled man, but the enormous head of a snarling bull. Two yellowed horns jut forth from its head, pointed and deadly. There's even a large gold ring through its nose.

"Is... is that a minotaur?" you stammer.

"Sort of," Finnegan says.

The creature glares down at you with glowing yellow eyes. Then it rears it head back and roars!

Finnegan lowers his head and shrugs. "Alright, yes. It's a minotaur."

57

58

The minotaur looks about to charge. Just then, Finnegan pulls a large grey object out of one of the open drawers. "Ah!" he cries triumphantly. "Found it!"

You edge closer to your friend, hoping he has some easy way out of this. Instead, he thrusts the object into your hands.

"Here," he tells you. "Hold this for a minute."

It's the figurine of a scaled, coiled dragon. You're not an expert, but it looks like it was carved from soapstone.

"Finny, what–"

"Kavalgyth, stop being such a baby!" shouts Finnegan. "A bet's a bet! You and I both know you lost fair and squ–"

The minotaur's eyes go a ferocious, bloodshot red. It lowers its head and charges!

You have three choices here, and none of them are spectacular.

If you want to stand your ground against the minotaur, grit your teeth and *TURN TO PAGE 42*

You can also attempt to reason with Kavalgyth. To try a diplomatic solution, *GO TO PAGE 104*

Of course, you can always take a page out of Sir Robin's book. To run away, *FLIP TO PAGE 89*

59

You quicken your pace as the tremors start up again. But then one of the slats beneath you breaks!

As one of your legs falls through, you dive forward. Your foot catches a solid plank and you manage to pull yourself back to your feet. But the world around you is still shaking. The shifting earth pulls the hand-ropes tight on both ends, and the tension threatens to shred the bridge to pieces!

You scramble for the opposite bank. Luckily you're traveling light, and are therefore fast. You reach the other end of the bridge just as the cables snap, sending the whole rotten thing into the yawning, sky-filled chasm.

Finally the tremors stop. As you lay on your back, gasping for breath, your vision begins going grey at the edges. You're afraid for a second you might pass out, but then you realize it's something even worse: the mist is closing in all around you!

You're on your feet in a second, spinning around as you look for a way out. A small corridor slices through the mist straight ahead of you. It's your only option. As the fog pushes in from behind, you bolt through the opening.

An enormous shadow emerges ahead. It's the tower! You run full speed, uncomfortably aware of the mist closing in on both sides. You have only seconds before it envelops you. There won't be anywhere to go.

Up ahead, details emerge. Two enormous oaken doors make up the entrance to the tower. One of them is cracked open. Light spills out from inside, silhouetting two figures standing in the doorway. Both of them are moving their arms hurriedly.

They seem to be beckoning you...

Can you make it inside before the mist collapses in on you?
FIND OUT OVER ON PAGE 123

60

The tower rumbles. The floor shakes. The diamond glows ever more brightly, as the booming overhead voice waits on your answer.

You stand there trying to make sense of the chaos. No one person or thing stands out! Out of everything you encountered there seemed to be no single thing – no common thread – that managed to weave everyone in the tower together...

It's therein that you find your answer.

"No one," you say aloud. "The tower *has* no master."

Your response is greeted by silence. The voice says nothing. Does nothing.

Suddenly a light flares. The beams emanating from the diamond grow sharper, more distinct. There's a high-pitched shriek as the tower's hum rises in pitch and volume, traversing through normal octaves and beyond the levels meant for human ears.

All at once, everything around you begins to fade!

You sprint for the center of the chamber. The diamond is a small, glowing sun. You can't even look at it directly. There's no time to think, or reason, or consider. You launch yourself forward and dive...

CLINK!

The diamond leaves the platform with a single, musical note. Its light goes out instantly, plunging the chamber into semi-darkness. Only the moonlight remains, cold and muted. Everything else is in shadow.

The tower shudders to a halt. The complete cessation of movement drives you to your knees. You look down, to where the jewel sits heavy in your hands. You expect to to be hot, even searing, but it's not even warm. Right now it looks completely dull and lifeless.

"*You did it,*" says a voice in your head. When you whirl around, YON is standing behind you.

"*You stopped the tower from blinking.*"

61

You rise slowly from the floor, on legs that still feel unsteady. YON approaches, and you notice he's blue now. He actually looks calm. Placid.

"I had to do it," you explain. "The tower was broken." You point at the fissure running through the diamond. "There's a–"

"*–a flaw in the focus jewel?*" YON finishes for you. "*Yes. There has been for quite some time. A very long while, actually.*"

You glance up through the skylight and breathe a sigh of relief. The stars are still there. Everything looks the same.

"*You are lucky,*" YON tells you. "*You could be looking up at a much different sky right now.*"

The light-being holds out one hand. Carefully you heft the diamond into it. For a brief moment it occurs to you that you're giving away a fortune.

"The tower moved at random because the diamond is cracked," you theorize. "Am I right?"

"*Yes.*" YON turns the jewel over in his hands, examining it from several different angles.

"And that's why it moved so often, too?"

"*Correct.*"

You stare back at YON. His many lights glimmer, reflecting back from within the deepest facets of the diamond. "You couldn't come here until now, could you?"

The light-being shakes his head. "*No,*" he answers. "*Not until you made it possible.*"

You walk in a slow circle around the shadowed room. Everything looks 'off'. All of the mirrors are dark.

"So what now?"

"*Now it begins,*" YON tells you. "*I will attempt the process of repairing the jewel. If, that is, I am able.*" A shiver runs through you. You don't even want to think about YON not being able to fix the tower. *"But first, I will need to move it to someplace neutral. Somewhere it will not be disturbed.*"

62

"Uhhh, no..." you say hesitantly. "That's not what I meant."

The light-being cocks his head at you quizzically.

"I meant, what about me?"

YON looks you dead in the eye, and you'd swear he actually grins. It's hard to tell without the light-being having a mouth.

"*Why I send you home first, of course.*"

Ten minutes later you're staring into a strange glowing gateway, produced when YON touched the focus jewel to one of the room's many mirrors. Everything inside looks very... orange.

"Are you sure about this?"

YON nods. "*It will take you back,*" he assures you. "*Beyond the tower, to where you need to be.*"

You shrug, thinking you might as well accept it. Traversing a magical orange portal wouldn't be the strangest thing that happened to you today.

"Uh, thanks YON," you say. "I appreciate–"

"*Please,*" your friend says with the wave of a hand. "*Because of your bravery, the denizens of the tower may all eventually go home. It is we who should be thanking you...*"

Back at the campsite, your fire is nearly gone. The tower blinked away minutes ago, off to wherever YON took it next.

As you think back to your adventure, a few lingering questions remain. Was there *really* a master of the tower? And the even bigger, more nagging mystery: *who wrote the letters?*

Some things, you realize, are better left unknown.

You conquered the Tower of Never There, and returned to tell the tale!

That itself is a very successful way to say

THE END

63

Still not sure why you're doing it, you approach the decrepit old rope bridge. Right away you notice it appears constructed of odd, mismatched materials. Its cables seem to made of some cross between plastic and wire, and the rotted planks are of a deep, rust-colored wood that you've never seen before.

The terrain looks foreign here too. The best way to describe it is if the ground simply doesn't belong; like the entire area was torn from somewhere else and just dropped here. If that's truly the case, it would explain why the bridge itself has been left at a dangerously uncomfortable angle.

Wistfully you glance back at the cobbled path. More and more, it seems like a wiser choice.

Still determined to cross the bridge? You're braver than I thought! *SKIP DOWN TO PAGE 145*

Then again, umm... maybe that path doesn't look so bad. Turn back and take it *OVER ON PAGE 33*

64

YON pulses bright red in the doorway. He extends one arm.

"*Come. There is nothing for you here.*"

As you allow YON to help you from the chamber, you notice he's pushed a second button. Another door lies open now. Beyond it, a new hallway.

"Thank you YON," you say gratefully.

The light being nods briefly before following you through the exit.

Time's getting short! Hurry on *OVER TO PAGE 179*

65

You pick up the pace. You're afraid to open your eyes too wide, but you're also afraid not to. If you wander off the path, you'll hurtle straight into the mist. And if you lose your sense of direction...

The rain is coming down harder now. You start to run. Panic sets in. And that's when you see it: the dark silhouette of the tower, looming just ahead.

"HEY!"

Was that a voice? Or was it just the storm? You wipe rain from your eyes and risk a quick glance. Two massive doors make up the entrance to the tower, at least three times as tall as you. One of them is partially open...

People!

Two slender figures stand in lighted doorway, nothing but shadows. They're motioning to you now, urging you inside. You lower your head, grit your teeth, and push yourself to run faster...

Will you make it? Only one way to find out! *TURN TO PAGE 123*

66

You follow Finnegan along another series of upward ramps. Eventually you're dumped into a large, open chamber lit by many torches. You must be up against the side of the tower, you realize, because one of the walls is open to the night sky.

"There he is!" Finny cries excitedly. Clapping his hand over his own mouth, he drops his voice down to a whisper. "Finally!"

"Who?"

"The boss man. The guy in charge." Finny shrugs one shoulder. "Sort of."

A stone ledge extends outside the tower. On it, you see the figure of a man. He stands there motionless, gazing into the stars. Right now his back is to you.

You however, are more focused on the sky. "It's dark outside!" you say with alarm. You wonder how long its been since you left your campsite. How much time you have left before the tower blinks...

"Forget about all that," Finnegan whispers. "He's not looking. We can get the jump on him!" Your friend rubs his hands together. "Oh, I got you where I want you now, big guy."

The man on the ledge doesn't appear big *or* threatening. In fact, he looks pretty ordinary.

"Why do we–"

You turn to Finny but he's not there. Your friend is already creeping along the chamber, his back pressed tightly to the wall. He motions you forward with him. "Come on," he hisses. "We need to tackle him now, before he turns around."

Do you follow Finnegan's lead and try to take the guy down? If so, *TURN TO PAGE 131*

Or maybe you feel like you need a little more information. If that's the case, *HEAD TO PAGE 83*

67

The ballerina is almost upon you. You're desperate to stop her!

Reaching into your things, you pull out the carved bone horn. Taking the deepest possible breath, you put it to your lips and blow.

The sound is low, deep, even haunting. Immediately you realize it was the wrong move.

The dancer becomes enraged! (How dare you so rudely interrupt her routine!) She spins into you full force, intentionally knocking you backward...

CRASH!

One of the tall windows – which has miraculously re-appeared behind you – shatters beneath your impact. Falling through it, you tumble out of the tower!

Down...

Down...

Down...

It's a long way to go, but you'll eventually reach

THE END

68

You have nothing to offer the dragon. Nothing to dissuade its attention from you. All you can do is stiffen. Freeze motionless, and hope for the best.

The creature shifts forward, its great bulk flowing with unnatural finesse. The dragon's arms end in taloned claws. Its teeth are jagged, two-foot stilettos dripping with saliva.

The dragon sniffs you. Curls itself around you. You can feel the scales rubbing against your body. The tip of its tail resting just beneath your chin.

You don't move.

You don't speak.

You don't even dare to breathe...

"YON..." you whisper finally. "YON!"

But there's no answer. There is no longer anyone around to help you. You don't even know where you are, or how you'll ever get back to where you were before. All you know is that you're completely at the serpent's mercy.

Maybe you should've explored more of the tower, took a few more chances. If so, you might've at least had something to try.

Sometimes bad luck is better than no luck at all. Especially in this case, where it happens to be

---

THE END

69

The taloned bat-thing comes on too fast! It dives like a bird of prey, leaving you no time to move!

Reacting instinctively, you throw up your arms to protect your face. Razor-sharp claws pierce the skin of your forearm, creating a long red cut from wrist to elbow.

You grab your injured arm and whirl, bracing for the next attack. But it never comes. The creature climbs high into the strange sky, makes three lazy circles, and then disappears.

Turning your attention back to your wound, it's nothing but bad news. Unfortunately the cut is both long *and* deep. You wrap it as best you can by stripping off your socks, even using one of them as a makeshift tourniquet. But you definitely can't continue. Not in this state.

As you turn your back to the tower, you can't help but wonder about all the discoveries you'll never get to make. Maybe one day you can come back again. Perhaps the tower will even be there for you...

As of right now though, this is

THE END

70

You wrack your brain, thinking of all the different characters you've met over the course of your adventure. One sticks out way more than all the rest...

"Finnegan!" you shout. "Finnegan must be master of the tower!"

There's a short pause, followed by deep, booming laughter:

HAHAHAHA! FINNEGAN? SURELY YOU MUST BE JOKING!

Your head drops. You feel bad enough at having blown it, but the laughter is making you feel even worse! But then the voice continues:

FINNEGAN IS BARELY THE MASTER OF TYING HIS OWN SHOES! EVEN SO, I FIND YOUR ANSWER AMUSING.

The tower trembles. The light in the center of the diamond has reached near-blinding levels.

CHOOSE ANOTHER.

Whoa, you're getting another shot! Don't mess up!

If you *know* who the master of the tower is, use the chart below to add up all the letters in that word. When you have the total you can *GO TO THAT PAGE*

A = 1	F = 6	K = 11	P = 16	U = 21	Z = 26
B = 2	G = 7	L = 12	Q = 17	V = 22	Example:
C = 3	H = 8	M = 13	R = 18	W= 23	ANNA =
D = 4	I = 9	N = 14	S = 19	X = 24	1+14+14+1
E = 5	J = 10	O = 15	T = 20	Y = 25	= 30

If you still don't know who the master is, *TURN TO PAGE 60*

71

The snake is almost on you. At the last moment you throw your arms wide.

"Sammy!"

The snake's head rears back at the mention of its name. You were right! It's definitely the same creature you met earlier – Kara's pet snake from the indoor garden. Only somehow, it's now much, much larger.

Sammy slides over to greet you, nuzzling up against your open hand. Finnegan looks awestruck.

"You *know* this snake?" he gasps.

"Uh, yeah," you say. "I guess I do." You're petting the creature with both hands now. When you start scratching the scales beneath Sammy's chin, he flicks out his forked tongue and licks your face like a dog!

"That's AWESOME!" Finnegan cries. Your friend is both delighted and impressed. After petting the snake himself, he points at something. A door has appeared on the other side of the room.

"Good boy Sammy," you tell the snake with a few final pats. "Gotta go now."

Incredibly the serpent seems to understand. It rubs against you playfully as it turns its massive body around. Then, nuzzling you one last time, it slithers back down the staircase.

"I underestimated you," Finny says admiringly. "Nice job!"

You heard what Finnegan said – Nice job! Now *GO TO PAGE 75*

72

Carefully you pull forth the beautiful crystal angel you found outside the tower. Although it's been less than an hour, that moment seems like forever ago.

You place it on its corresponding pedestal and step back. And it's a good thing you do.

Almost immediately, the figurine begins to change. It grows, twists, and morphs into something larger than itself. Eventually it's a full-blown angel, even bigger than you!

The angel looks down at you. She's strikingly beautiful. Then she smiles... and her grin twists grotesquely around a mouthful of broken teeth!

With a shriek and a laugh, the angel launches herself into the air. Her wings open and she begins beating them, climbing and swooping in the air above you. The domed ceiling is huge. She has plenty of room.

Then, without warning, she dives!

There's no time to think, or talk, or do anything else but duck! The angel swoops over you in a low arc, narrowly missing your head before climbing back into the upper dome. She almost took your face off... but when you look back, she's laughing!

The angel is coming around for another pass. You have to stop her!

If you have the Lotus Blossom you can try offering it to her *ON PAGE 129*

If you have the Jeweled Pin you can give her that instead by *HEADING TO PAGE 87*

If you have the Bone Horn, blow it and see what happens *BACK ON PAGE 31*

If you have the Snow Globe you can shake it up and *GO TO PAGE 43*

If you have none of these things, *FLIP DOWN TO PAGE 178*

73

You're halfway through the door when you feel someone grab you. A man pulls you into the next room, peers down at you, and grins.

"Ah, you're finally here! Took you long enough!" He snatches up your hand and shakes it so vigorously your arm nearly comes off. "I'm Finnegan. Finny, for short."

"I– I'm Tyler."

Finnegan nods. "No time for that right now." He glances hurriedly over his shoulder. "Were you followed?"

"Followed?"

"Never mind. Come with me, quickly!" Before you can say another word Finnegan ducks into another chamber. You follow, and end up in what looks like a large, open foyer. He slams the door closed behind you the second you're through.

"You're *sure* you weren't followed?" he asks again.

"No. I mean, I'm pretty sure I wasn't." He squints as if he doesn't believe you. "Why? Who's chasing you?"

"Him."

You look around, half expecting to see someone. You don't. In a snap decision, you decide to play along. "Okay... why is *he* chasing you?"

Finnegan laughs. "Why does he do anything? He's crazy!" The man's eyes shift from side to side. "Or maybe he's a just a genius. Or even a crazy genius. Those two things usually go hand in hand, you know." Finny stops to check his watch. "Wow. It's one-thirty. We'd better get going."

"One thirty?" you repeat. It doesn't seem right to you. "Wait, does time pass in here the same as it does out there?"

Finnegan shrugs. "Dunno. But I *always* like to know what time it is."

You're confused. No... actually it's way beyond that. Confusion might even be an improvement right now. "I don't even know where I am!" you cry suddenly. "Or who you are. Or why I'm here! Heck, *you* don't even know what–"

"You're here to go up, right?" Finny asks out of the blue.

You pause for a long moment. Eventually you nod your head.

"Well I'm your guy!" Finnegan declares. He slaps you on the shoulder and winks. "Come on then, let's go. We don't have a lot of time."

Are you crazy enough to follow Finnegan? Find out *OVER ON PAGE 99*

74

You choose the upward-sloping passage, hoping it will take you to the surface. Right away you feel like you made the right choice. The air tastes fresher, cleaner. You can even feel a breeze.

But the bats are still flying all around you. Most use their radar to avoid you, but a few unlucky ones smash into you with the very unpleasant crunch of tiny bat bones.

Eventually you see the proverbial light at the end of the tunnel: there's an opening in the opposite end! You pick up the pace and head toward it, waving your arms wildly in front of you. As you burst forth from the cavern the massive tower is right there. It looms over you like a dark giant.

An enormous set of double doors make up the tower entrance. One is open, and light spills forth from inside. Framed in the doorway are the silhouettes of two people. One of them is frantically waving an arm, beckoning you inside...

Quick! Get into the tower before anything else happens! *TURN TO PAGE 123*

75

The next chamber of the tower is painted red and black. A strange, sourceless light emanates from somewhere overhead, throwing a weird amber pall over everything beneath it.

Located in the dead center of the room is a tall, wicked-looking statue.

"What's that?" you ask.

Finnegan shakes his head. For once he says nothing.

You approach it cautiously. The statue could be of a man, or a woman, or of neither. Tall and twisted, it has an eerie, otherworldly feel to it. It also looks impossibly smooth, almost like liquid. You're tempted to reach out and touch it.

"What do you think it's made of?"

Finny looks back at you solemnly. "*I'm* not touching it."

As disquieting as it appears, the statue's surface is oddly inviting. You get closer, and notice it also seems to radiate warmth.

"There's something written on the back," you say. "Boost me up. I might be able to read it."

Your friend still hasn't moved. His expression is grave.

"Maybe we should skip this one, boss."

Finnegan's obviously not going to help you here. If you want to read the statue's inscription, you're going to have to climb it.

If you climb the statue, *HEAD ON BACK TO PAGE 27*

If you think Finny might be right, avoid the whole thing by *TURNING TO PAGE 66*

76

You press the button with the crossed swords. It slides deeply into the wall, so much in fact that a small opening above the button is revealed, and an object drops out.

"Whoa!"

Luckily you have the reflexes of a hockey goalie (or at least that's what you've always told yourself!) You reach out and catch the object before it hits the floor.

It's a small carved figurine. A soldier, crafted from smoothly-polished ebony wood.

"What's this about?" you ask YON. But the light-being only stares back at you impassively.

CLICK!

Another door grinds open in the center of a blank wall. You tuck the figurine into your pocket and check it out. A small hallway ends in a 'Y'-shaped corridor, leaving you with two choices.

If you take the LEFT fork, *TURN TO PAGE 113*
If you take the RIGHT fork, *GO TO PAGE 179*

77

You jump!

Annnnd.... you fall.

You fall a long, long way through the darkness, feeling nothing, seeing nothing on your way down. For a brief instant you feel something brush past your face, and then...

Well... you know.

Did you *really* just follow Finnegan off the side of a perfectly good bridge? And hey, didn't your mother warn you against things like that?

Well, what's done is done. And right now this is unquestionably

---

THE END

78

You pick up the golden orb and place it on the stand. The strange figure shimmers for a moment, and then every one of its lights turn gold.

"*I am YON*," a voice booms. It seems to come from within your head. You realize the figure – or creature, or whatever it is – has no mouth, or even a face. "*You are to come with me.*"

The golden figure strides from the room without waiting for an answer. With nothing else to do, you follow.

"Are... are you my guide now?"

"*I am YON*," the creature repeats. You notice its lights twinkle brightly as it 'speaks'. Somehow, it also moves without noise. "*I am only to–*"

The voice in your head cuts off as you're distracted by the next room. Here, a large yawning window opens into the night sky. You rush over to it – probably a bit too quickly – and are overcome with vertigo.

The ground is at least a thousand feet below!

"We're so high!" you gasp. Instinctively you take a step backward. The arched window, long and wide, is stretched way too close to the floor for your liking.

YON says nothing as you peer into the darkness. Down below you see the mountains, the trees, the snow-frosted ridge where you set up your camp. You swear you can even see a lazy curl of smoke winding its way up from your fire.

"We have to be near the top," you reason. "Right?"

Suddenly, everything changes. You see things outside that don't make any sense. Different landscapes flash by. The world outside the window seems familiar, then foreign... even alien at times.

"Did the tower blink?" you ask in alarm.

"*No*," the voice booms. "*But it will soon.*"

The mountains twist into pockmarked hills, in bizarre shapes you could've never conceived. The horizon melts into a rolling green ocean. It becomes a reaching red desert. A lake of fire...

"*You are seeing images of places it has been*," YON explains. "*These are reflections only. Like ghosts.*"

As you turn you notice YON is twice as close to you as before. Not being able to hear him move is getting a little uncomfortable.

You glance back through the window. Everything is foggy, hazy. It's like a sheer curtain has dropped, and all sorts of images are being projected onto it. Yet if you concentrate hard enough, you can still see through to the other side.

"I need to find out who brought me here," you say. "And then I need to leave."

The golden figure cocks its head at you. "*You mean you still don't know?*"

You squint back at him. *Was that a smirk where YON'S mouth should be?*

"No," you say. "I mean yes. I mean, I really don't–"

YON edges closer. "*Look there*," he points.

"Where?"

The being of light is right behind you now, his arm going over your shoulder. "*See that on the horizon?*"

You squint again. Seeing nothing, you shake your head.

"*The light in here may be obscuring your vision*," YON says. "*Perhaps if you leaned out a bit, into the darkness, your eyes would adjust. Then you will see.*"

What does YON see out there? You can lean further out into the darkness by *GOING TO PAGE 17*

On the other hand, maybe you should forget about the window entirely. You can do that by *TURNING TO PAGE 52*

80

You think back to everything you've seen in your time here. Mirrors. Twins. Images of yourself.

You consider the way that others here have treated you. The familiarity. The strange, nagging feeling you've *been here* before...

"TYLER!" you answer loudly. "The master of the tower is *myself*."

There's a long, drawn-out pause, and then the rumbling stops. The tower is no longer shaking.

"Did you hear me?" you shout defiantly. "*I am* the master of the tower!"

A brash, ringing sound assails your ears. You spin around, and something catches your eye.

Off to the side of the room, one of the mirrors is glowing.

You approach cautiously. A golden yellow light originates from *inside* the mirror. As you get closer, you notice a figure is in there.

That figure is you.

You swallow a lump in your throat. The Tyler on the other side of the glass does not. He merely stands there facing you, staring you down. You also notice he's holding something in one hand...

The diamond.

The you in the mirror is holding another version of the diamond mounted directly behind you. Only *his* diamond is perfect. Flawless. There's not a single blemish on it.

You hold out your hand. Nothing happens. The other you doesn't move, doesn't react to your own movement.

The Tyler in the mirror appears to be waiting for something...

Alright, you're down to two your last two options! Which do you choose?

You can reach out and touch the surface of the mirror. If this is your choice, *TURN TO PAGE 152*

You can also pick something up and use it to smash the mirror. To try that option, *FLIP TO PAGE 39*

81

The dragon hovers over you! But what does it want?

Gold? Jewels?

Thinking fast, you remove the exquisite jeweled pin Kara gave you earlier. The colorful gemstones sparkle, even in the dim light.

The dragon pauses. It leans in to consider your offering, so close to your face that its breath nearly knocks you over! Scaled lips peel back over jagged, razor-sharp teeth. The creature shifts forward, claws digging deeply into the soft earth...

Perhaps deciding you'd be good to have around, the dragon sweeps you up with one arm! There's no chance to struggle as it springs into the night sky, flapping powerful wings as it flies far and away from wherever you happened to be.

Know what dragons like even better than treasure? Playmates. Squatting around in a lair all day can get extremely boring!

Looks like you're stuck as one, at least for now. Which makes this

---

THE END

82

Something in Kara's voice is just too convincing. Rather than swing at the snake, you stay your hand.

Sure enough, the snake doesn't strike. Kara extends one hand and it slides up her arm, finally coming to rest coiled around one shoulder. She smiles at the snake, causing it to flick its tongue in and out rapidly. It actually looks happy.

"This is Sammy," Kara says. "He's my friend!"

You turn to Una, who is still standing in utter astonishment. Kara rolls her eyes in frustration.

"I told you all about him," she says, poking her sister. "Remember?" She's stroking the top of the snake's head now. "He's harmless!"

"You named your snake *Sammy?*" is all Una can say. "Sammy the snake?"

"Stop it," Kara admonishes. "You'll hurt his feelings!"

The blue-eyed sister is covering the snake's ears now. Which of course makes you wonder, *do snakes even* have *ears?*

Kara holds Sammy out so you can pet him, which you do. Snakes have never bothered you. In fact, you and most animals have always been pretty cool.

"See?" Kara jeers at Una. Gently she places Sammy down in the tall grass. He flicks out his forked tongue a few more times before slithering away. "Come on, we'd better get Tyler where he needs to go."

Continue through the garden *OVER ON PAGE 148*

"Finny..." you whisper. But your friend doesn't respond. He's still moving forward, padding silently toward the ledge.

"*FINNEGAN!*"

He whirls and shoots you a dirty look. Silently he mouths the word "*What?*"

"I'm not jumping some strange guy," you tell him, "just because you have a vendetta!"

Finnegan winces at the volume of your voice. After a quick look over his shoulder he makes a shushing motion with his finger.

"No," you tell him. "Don't shush me. I don't have time for this. Whoever that guy is, we have to leave him alone. I've already been here too long!"

Your friend's shoulders slump in disappointment. But only for a second. Finally he slinks back over to where you're standing.

"Okay, okay," he says placatingly. He glances back again. "Besides, we missed our moment." You look back and see that he's right. The ledge is now empty against the twinkling sky. "You spooked him," Finnegan tells you.

You're too frustrated to argue. "Fine," you agree. "I spooked him. Where the heck did he go anyway?"

Finny stares back at you for a long moment. He doesn't answer.

"Alright, let's move," Finnegan says. He jabs a finger upward in the direction of your goal. "The good news is you're almost there."

There's another steep staircase leading up and out of here. Take it *OVER ON PAGE 112*

84

You grab at the mud tentacles, but there's nothing to hold onto! The mud is soft, slippery. It glides through your hands and squishes out between your fingers. Yet somehow, somewhere within each tendril, there's enough strength and tension to keep you pinned.

Kara is shouting something, but you don't know what. One of the larger tentacles is wrapped around your head now. Your ears are covered. Your eyes. The harder you fight, the worse it gets. You're sinking fast...

You're almost up to your neck when the pulling stops. The tendrils release you, but by then you're planted firmly in the mud, arms pinned at your sides.

"We're going to be okay," Kara says faintly. There's barely any air in her lungs. You're all so constricted by the mud it's tough to speak. "They're done with us for now."

"*Done* with us?" you grunt. "How do you know?"

"Well... this might've happened to me once before," the blue-eyed sister admits.

"This *happened* to you once before?" Una groans. You can see she's pinned deepest of all, practically up to her chin.

"Okay, maybe twice," Kara relents. "They're not malicious, really. I think they just like us here." She spits a piece of mud out before continuing. "Eventually everything will get soft enough that we can wiggle our way free."

"How long?" you and Una both say in stereo.

"Not long," Kara says. "Two, three hours tops."

Hours?

Your body isn't the only thing sunk, because now your heart sinks too. You always thought getting home would be a forgone conclusion. But now you're realizing this might be

THE END

"Twins!" you cry out, into the seemingly open air. "The answer is *twins.*"

Your voice echoes loudly in the cold stone chamber. For a moment nothing happens. Then, just as you're wondering if you spoke the wrong answer, a high-pitched twinkling sound reaches your ears.

The glass directly beneath you shimmers. It goes from partially frosted over to totally crystal clear. Frightened, you leap back. There's a man on the other side!

He looks like you. In every aspect, every way, the man is a mirror image of yourself. He stands on the other side of the floor, looking up at you just as you look down at him. Then he smiles...

... and fades away.

The glass floor is opaque again. You're standing on it open-mouthed, unable to speak.

"YON..." you say when you find your voice again. "What was–"

But the light-being has already ducked beneath the archway. He gestures back at you with an open palm.

"*Come,*" YON's voice registers inside your head. "*You are finally here.*"

Finally here? Finally *where?* Find out when you *TURN TO PAGE 20*

86

The pink mist swirls around your ankles. It reaches your knees, your thighs...

YON flashes brightly. He steps up, seizes the doorknob, and turns it in the opposite direction.

It opens.

"*Get inside*," YON orders. He doesn't have to tell you twice.

Still covering your mouth, you rush through the open door. YON slams it shut behind you. Remnants of the pink mist trail briefly into the room before dissipating.

"Thanks," you cough. YON nods.

"And hey, I thought you weren't supposed to help me?"

The light-being flashes crimson. He pulses twice before answering.

"*I have been doing everything I am supposed to do*," YON says, "*for far too long*." As you watch, his body language changes. His chin drops. His shoulders slump. "*And yet still I am here*."

His tone has you overcome with sadness. It takes everything you have to resist reaching out and putting a hand on his shoulder.

Your friend turns and leaves through an exit, where another set of steps climbs upward. "*Come*," YON says. "*You are near the top*."

Near the top? Nice! *FLIP TO PAGE 150*

87

The angel comes around for a second pass. Maybe she wants something. She *has* to want something!

Fumbling with the clasp, you remove the exquisite jeweled pin that Kara gave you earlier. Hey, it's jewelry. It's exquisite. How could a semi-beautiful angel like this one *not* like it?

THWAP!

The angle smacks the pin from your hand so fast you don't even know where it went! There's a quick flash of color, and a split second later the pin goes spinning off into the darkness.

Uh oh. Guess that didn't work! Better try something else...

Whoa! Here she comes again... and she doesn't look happy!

If you have the Lotus Blossom you can try giving it to her *ON PAGE 129*

If you have the Bone Horn, try blowing into it *BY TURNING TO PAGE 31*

If you have the Snow Globe, shake it as hard as you can *OVER ON PAGE 43*

If you have none of these things, *FLIP DOWN TO PAGE 178*

88

The gems are too tempting. And the beetle looks harmless! Being cautious is one thing, but in this case you'd be stupid *not* to grab them.

Before Finnegan can say another word you jam your hand in the tank...

Uh oh.

The beetle's head explodes! Or rather, its head blows up to five times normal size in the span of half a second. This leaves you no time to move, no time to react as the insect's jaws flap open, revealing row after row of razor-sharp teeth!

Your hand isn't just bitten – it's consumed. It disappears entirely into the creature's maw, straight up to the thorax, and that's where you get the unique experience of being punctured with a thousand serrated needles all at once.

Thankfully, unconsciousness sets in *way* before the debilitating pain of the poison does...

You wake up in what *has* to be Finnegan's room – a mis-moshed, multi-world collection of the most gaudy and colorful furnishings ever conceived. Your hand – if it's even still in there – is swaddled in a thick mountain of bandages.

"Hey," Finny smiles merrily. "Welcome back."

Your attention is drawn to the window, where a strange landscape of molten green rock flows by. There are rivers of the stuff moving in every direction, stretching as far as the eye can see.

"The tower blinked, didn't it?" you say sullenly.

"Yes, but cheer up," Finnegan says. "The tower blinks a lot. We'll be back in your neck of the woods before you know it. No time at all, really."

"Really?"

"Well, no, not really," Finny admits. "But one day... maybe eventually..."

Whoops. Greed hurts. Sometimes even more than a thousand needles.

Looks like this is

THE END

89

"Run!" you shout.

Finnegan wastes no time arguing. He points to a back exit along the far wall, and together you rush through. The minotaur is picking up speed. It's still coming!

"Hang on," Finny says casually.

You turn, just in time to see the creature spring at your friend with two powerful legs. It goes sailing through the air, straight at Finnegan...

... and then he slams the door in its face!

The wooden exit door is totally obliterated. Hanging through, half in and half out of the room, is the unconscious, crumpled-up form of Kavalgyth the minotaur.

"He's big, but he never was smart," Finnegan says. He makes the double hand-wiping motion in the air of a job well done. "Now lets go, before he wakes up."

That sounds like the best idea you've heard all day. You follow Finny through corridors and chambers, climbing up ramps and staircases as you ascend through the tower. Eventually, when you're far enough from the minotaur's room that you feel comfortable, you pull out the figurine of the soapstone dragon.

"Here," you say, holding it out. But Finny shakes his head.

"Nah, you keep it," he tells you. "That thing has brought me nothing but bad luck!"

Bad luck? Why in the world would *you* want it then?

Never mind. Tuck the dragon figurine in your pocket and *HEAD TO PAGE 138*

90

Thinking back to everyone – and everything – you encountered during your time here, one of the tower's occupants stands out as having the most commanding presence.

"The sphinx!" you cry out. "The sphinx *must* be the master!"

An uncomfortable silence passes. You begin to wonder if the voice even heard you. Then:

THE SPHINX IS WISE. IT IS THE MASTER OF BOTH KNOWLEDGE AND ENLIGHTENMENT.

There's a slight pause before it finishes speaking.

BUT IT IS AS MUCH A PRISONER AS ALL THE OTHERS.

You let out a long, disappointed sigh. So close! But still...

The tower is shaking visibly now. The mirrors around the chamber waver as they reflect the brightness of the diamond, which is growing into a blinding white light.

All of a sudden the voice speaks again:

YOU MAY CHOOSE ANOTHER.

Sweet, you get to pick again! But do you have another guess in you?

If you *know* who the master of the tower is, use the chart below to add up all the letters in that word. When you have the total you can *GO TO THAT PAGE*

A = 1	F = 6	K = 11	P = 16	U = 21	Z = 26
B = 2	G = 7	L = 12	Q = 17	V = 22	Example:
C = 3	H = 8	M = 13	R = 18	W = 23	ANNA =
D = 4	I = 9	N = 14	S = 19	X = 24	1+14+14+1
E = 5	J = 10	O = 15	T = 20	Y = 25	= 30

If you're still not sure who the master is, *TURN TO PAGE 60*

91

You're not sure how much longer you can go on avoiding the creature. It seems to get faster as it grows ever more angry, and you're already getting tired.

"Here!" Finny yells. "Kavalgyth, HERE!"

Your friend is holding up a very exotic – and very fragile-looking – glass orb. You notice a whole collection of such orbs spread out across the mantle of the fireplace.

Finnegan's voice gives the minotaur pause. For the first time, it stops.

"I'll smash it!" Finny threatens. "Don't think I won't!" He locks eyes with you and jerks his head in the direction of a back exit. "I'll shatter it into a million pieces!"

Kavalgyth roars. He starts toward Finnegan, but now he's moving a lot more cautiously. You can tell the orb is very valuable to him.

The two of you continue edging toward the door. When you're finally at the threshold, Finnegan rears his arm back and fires the orb directly over the minotaur's head.

You never know whether the creature catches it or not. You're too busy running! Corridors and ramps lead you ever upward, through the tower, as Kavalgyth's screams fade into the distance. Finally you stop, doubled over with exertion, at the top of a long staircase.

"That... was... stupid..." you gasp between breaths.

"I know, right?" Finny agrees. "I mean, who in the world smashes his own stool?"

The fun with Finnegan continues *OVER ON PAGE 138*

92

You flounder across the outside ledge, trying frantically to regain your balance. Only ten feet separates you from the edge! Four feet! Two...

At the last possible second you throw yourself to the ground, allowing friction to stop your momentum. Pain flares as your body skids across hard stone... but you make it!

You recover quickly and scramble to your feet. There's no sign of the man on the ledge. All you see is Finnegan, rushing to your aid. Much too late, of course.

"You missed him, eh?" Finny asks.

"Obviously." A more sarcastic reply comes to mind, but you're too busy taking in the view. You're very high up now, and also shivering. The wind is whipping hard against your skin.

"We'll get him next time," Finnegan tells you. "Come on back inside. I found the stairs."

Get in out of the cold when you *FLIP TO PAGE 112*

93

Kara's eyes are too sad and convincing. You can't resist. Reaching up, you pluck the beautiful flower.

"Here you go," you say, presenting her with the rainbow blossom. Kara squeals with joy. She tucks the flower into her hair, pinning it behind one ear.

"Umm... Tyler," Una says. There's something very unsettling about her voice. She points to your wrist. "Look."

A tiny droplet of blood is running down your forearm. You glance back at the vine and notice it's covered with strangely hooked thorns.

Kara's smile dissolves instantly away. Her face is painted with worry.

"It's just a scratch," you tell them, smiling to show everything's okay. "It's not... anything... to be worrr..."

You feel sick. Dizzy. Nauseous.

"The thorns!" cries Una.

A cold, icy sensation inches along your veins as the flower's toxin takes hold. Your extremities begin to tingle. Your legs feel like they're no longer there, and suddenly you're looking up from the ground.

"Tyler!"

The last thing you see are the two girls standing over you, arguing about whose fault this is. Then you fade into unconsciousness, making this

THE END

94

The smoke is starting to get to you. All of a sudden you're exhausted, and the next thing you know you're sitting on the floor.

I'll just rest for a moment, you think to yourself. *Get my strength back...*

When you look up again you're in a field. Everything is mud and muck. Steam rises from the warm ground as men swarm all around you. They are armed, armored. But none of them pay you any attention.

The scene changes. Now there's a battle. Two armies clash on a great hill, looking down over a raging river. Soldiers run back and forth, barking orders, some passing only a few feet away from you.

You try to stand, but can't. You're just too tired. A horn blows...

The braying of the horn is deep, resonant. It echoes off the hill and reverberates through the battlefield. Almost immediately the soldiers of an entire army break and run. One by one they begin to retreat, and the vision fades...

Snap out of it and *TURN TO PAGE 163*

95

You stare at the sign for a while, then down at the letters in your hand. 'DANGER' certainly makes sense, but the extra 'E' still bothers you. Then, like a bolt of lightning, it hits you!

"Got it!"

Walking forward, you tack the fallen letters back onto the sign. Using every last one of them, it now spells:

ANGERED

"Angered?" Una asks. "What could be down that path that's angered?"

You don't really expect an answer, but then Kara's expression takes on one of sudden enlightenment. "Wait!" she says. "Stay right here!"

She dashes down the left-hand path, turns a corner, and disappears from sight. Una appears worried. After an awkward minute the two of you exchange anxious looks, but then much to your relief Kara comes sprinting back. The blue-eyed sister is holding something in her hands now. It's small and scaly and looks sort of like a baby iguana. Except for the fact it's flaming red.

"The Saspernink!" Kara explains. She's petting the creature gently now. But instead of cooing, the tiny lizard opens its gullet and lets out a tremendous roar!

"How could that thing be so loud?" you wince. "And why is it angry?"

"Oh it's not," Kara says. "Angry, that is. It's very happy right now." She strokes its back. "Whoever put the sign up probably didn't know that."

You have to admit the creature is cute. Unconsciously you reach out and start petting it too. It lifts its chin to give you better access.

Una still hasn't taken her hands from her ears. "Stop petting it!"

"It won't roar again," Kara assures her. "It's just a defense mechanism. That, and the powerful musk it excretes through its skin."

You jerk your hand back and reluctantly bring it to your nose. It smells strong and musty. "Wish you'd told me that before I touched it!"

Kara laughs. "Yeah, whoops."

Head down the right side path by *TURNING TO PAGE 30*

96

There's a whole lot of tower left to explore, you reason. A key might come in handy later, especially if something is locked.

"Stay here," you tell the girls. "I'll be right back."

Still wondering if you're crazy, you move into the darker part of the forest. The spiderwebs are everywhere. You keep an ear cocked, listening for a rustle or a chittering or whatever sound it is that giant spiders would make. You hear nothing.

Eventually you arrive at the key. Wishing you had your knife, you grab hold of it and being pulling it free. It resists at first, but eventually comes loose with a much-too-loud ripping and tearing sound.

Suddenly the key comes free! It flies out of your hand and lands in the grass!

Beside you, the web still quivers and shakes. You wince hard and expect the worst...

For once nothing happens. Thankfully, no spiders drop down from the trees.

"Wow," Kara says when you return to the path. "That's gorgeous!" She runs a thumb over the top of the key. "Is that an octopus?"

"Yes," you say, counting the eight tentacles. "It sure is."

The silver key feels heavy in your hand, and oddly warm. You slip it into your pocket.

"Come on," says Una. "We're almost to the end of the garden."

See that? Sometimes being brave pays off! Other times however...

Keep moving down the path when you *TURN TO PAGE 148*

98

You unclasp the jeweled pin Kara gave you in the bottom level of the tower. Holding it out, you offer it to the soldier.

CLANG!

The tip of the broadsword strikes the pin with deadly accuracy. It goes spinning into the shadows! Fearfully you check your hand...

Whew! You still have five fingers.

"Listen," you plead to the warrior. "If you could just give me a minute to explain–"

The soldier answers by butting you hard with his shield. You fall backward, off balance, and go crashing to the floor!

"Wait!"

The warrior follows up with a downward chop. With no time to spare, you roll out of the way...

Better hurry... you're running out of time (and options)!

If you own the Lotus Blossom you can try giving it to the soldier *ON PAGE 32*

If you own the Bone Horn you can try blowing it by *TURNING TO PAGE 51*

If you own the Snow Globe, shake it as hard as you can and *FLIP TO PAGE 144*

If you have none of these things, *TURN TO PAGE 168*

Finnegan leads you into a very long hallway with many doors. You count at least twelve on each side, and that's only as far as you can see.

"How big is this place?" you breathe. "I mean–"

But Finny is no longer by your side. He sprints up to one of the doors on the left and begins pounding on it with his fist. "I SAID BE QUIET IN THERE!" he screams.

You heard nothing.

"How many times do I have to tell them?" Finnegan demands. He looks at you and rolls his eyes. "It never ends."

Suddenly there's noise. Shouts and cries ring out from the opposite side of the hallway, followed by boisterous laughter. It's all coming from a different door. "What about them?" you ask.

Finny blinks. "What about who?"

You sigh. "Never mind." You look the hallway up and down. "Okay, so which door?"

"Doors?" asks Finnegan. "Oh, you don't want any of *these* doors." He leans in close, putting one hand to the side of his mouth. "*Trust me*," he says confidentially.

You surrender, dropping your hands to your sides. "Then what?"

"Well you said you wanted to go up, right?" Finny says. "Stairs or elevator?"

If you'd like to take the stairs, *TURN TO PAGE 16*

If you'd rather take the elevator, *GO TO PAGE 169*

100

The platform lifts you to dizzying new heights, pushing you ever closer to the domed ceiling. Just as you're afraid of being crushed an opening appears, and you're guided through into the very topmost chamber of the tower.

The room is made almost entirely of glass. The rounded walls are a mixture of stone and marble, with small angular mirrors set throughout. Silver moonlight filters down from a gigantic, multi-faceted skylight above.

You're at the top!

Looking back toward the middle of the room, you gasp. On a platform in the dead center of the chamber is a huge diamond. It's roughly the size of a grapefruit!

Light streams in through the skylight, which you can see now is angled to focus on the diamond. The facets of the jewel reflect the light out in every direction, splashing it all over the inside of the chamber. It bounces from the mirrors, creating an even greater effect.

Reverently you follow the light beams. Pinpricks of brightness illuminate the walls, focusing and coalescing into all different shapes and patterns. They form beautiful, intricate maps over the curved inner surface of the tower.

No, not maps, you think.

Star maps.

"This is how the tower travels," you breathe aloud. You reach out to touch a smooth wall and light sparkles along the back of your hand. "This shows exactly where it goes. *When* it goes..."

As if intruding upon your very thoughts, the tower rumbles! You feel the beginnings of vibration beneath your feet. A low, steady hum...

101

You look back at the diamond. Very slowly, it's begun to revolve. But then you notice something else: the diamond isn't perfect.

It's cracked.

You move in for a closer look. A long, jagged fissure runs the entire length of the gemstone. A series of smaller cracks also spider out from the main imperfection. These change the way the light plays as it leaves the big jewel.

The hum grows louder, the vibrations more pronounced. The diamond, you notice, also seems to be gathering light.

Your mind reels. You're at a loss for what to do! The tower is coming to life beneath your feet. It's only moments away from blinking...

Suddenly a voice rings out! It booms loudly from all around you, filling the stone and glass chamber with its deep, almost musical resonance.

The voice poses a single, thundering question:

WHO IS THE MASTER OF THE TOWER?

The hum grows louder. The tower is shaking. You stand trembling in utter bewilderment, with only seconds to answer...

This is it! Your big moment! Are you going to shine? Or will you blow it!

If you *know* who the master of the tower is, use the chart below to add up all the letters in that word. When you have the total you can *GO TO THAT PAGE*

A = 1	F = 6	K = 11	P = 16	U = 21	Z = 26
B = 2	G = 7	L = 12	Q = 17	V = 22	Example:
C = 3	H = 8	M = 13	R = 18	W = 23	ANNA =
D = 4	I = 9	N = 14	S = 19	X = 24	1+14+14+1
E = 5	J = 10	O = 15	T = 20	Y = 25	= 30

If you don't know who the master of the tower might be, *TURN TO PAGE 60*

102

The very last thing that interests you right now is exploring some dank, creepy cave. Better to stick to the path. The tower can't be far away.

You move quickly but cautiously, listening for any hint of that booming sound again. For a while you hear nothing, but then there's a distant rumble. The sky changes. Dark grey clouds roll in, swirling angrily above you.

The forest comes to an end. There's another clearing, and standing in the middle is the tower. It's tall and dark, but for some reason, not ominous.

Rain starts to fall. It pelts you hard, and the droplets are freezing. As you quicken your pace, lightning flashes. Once, twice, then three and four times. You move even faster.

To your dismay, the bolts are getting closer! One strikes the ground beside the tower, sending a shower of dirt and rock into the air. You're running now. The bolts strike closer and with more frequency, slamming down in the clearing all around you!

Up ahead, the massive oaken doors to the tower are cracked open. Warm light streams from inside. Two young women are silhouetted in the doorway, beckoning you inside with with a frantic motion of their arms.

All around you the lightning strikes harder and nearer than ever before! There's a large tree at the very edge of the clearing. Maybe you could duck back beneath it and take shelter until the storm passes.

Then again, you're almost there...

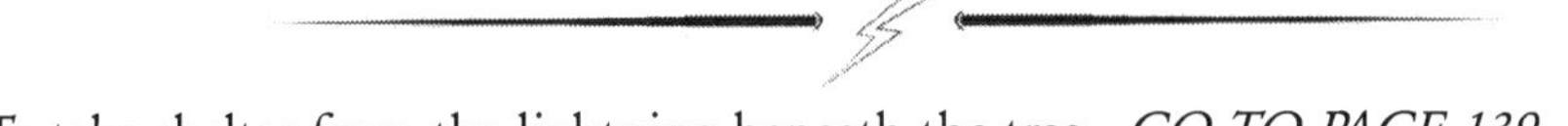

To take shelter from the lightning beneath the tree, *GO TO PAGE 139*

If you still think you can make the tower, *SPRINT AHEAD TO PAGE 123*

103

It's no use! The door won't open and there's no other way out. By now the mist is so thick you can't even see to go backward. Retreat is impossible.

The strange fog keeps rising. It envelops your face, choking you..

The last thing you see is YON. A vague gold blur, his brightness level fades in and out as he pulsates rapidly. He might even be laughing!

You clutch your chest as you sink to the floor. Everything is rose-colored now. Everything smells sweet.

Your eyes slowly close as you accept this is likely

THE END

104

With agility you didn't realize you possess, you throw yourself to one side of the bedroom. The minotaur sails past you in a blur of wind.

"Now Kavalgyth," you say, trying to wrap your tongue around the creature's strange name. You're holding your hands out in front of you, palms up. "Listen... we didn't mean to–"

The minotaur whirls and snorts. It rushes again. This time you scramble under the bed, rolling your body like a spinning log until you come out the other side.

You pop up. "Kavalgyth! Listen!"

The bull-creature's eyes are murderous. It picks up a stool from a nearby desk and smashes it against the floor. One of the chair's shattered legs is the only thing left in the minotaur's hand. It's as thick as a baseball bat and jagged at the broken end.

"I think he's mad," Finny says. The minotaur charges at you again. "He's *always* mad," Finnegan adds.

Looks like negotiations aren't going so well. Better flip two coins!

If both coins turn up HEADS when you flip them *TURN TO PAGE 158*

If they both land on TAILS instead, *FLIP BACK TO PAGE 36*

If you get one each of HEADS and TAILS, cross your fingers, cross your toes, and *GO TO PAGE 91*

105

The path ends at a large pool of cool, clear water. From what you can see, it picks up again on the other side.

"This place is unbelievable," you say, scanning around. "I can't believe you have an indoor *pond.*"

"That's nothing," Kara replies. "You should see our ocean."

"Your *what?*"

Una shoots her sister a glance and Kara bursts out laughing. "I'm kidding, I'm kidding," she giggles. "But I totally had you there, right?"

You turn four shades of red, but you laugh anyway. "Maybe."

Una raises an arm. "We can skirt around the water in this direction," she points. "It's the shortest way to get back on the path."

"Nah uh," Kara shakes her head. "The shortest way is *through* the water. It's only knee-deep." She looks over at you and shrugs. "You want to save time, right?"

You've got another fun choice to make here!

You can avoid the pond by skirting its edge *OVER ON PAGE 133*

Or you can wade through the pond to save time *BACK ON PAGE 37*

106

You dive left... and...
CRUNCH!

Starboard means *right*. Port side is left. Good to know for next time, but right now this is

---

THE END

107

You think back to the minotaur you met in the heart of the tower. So strong. So powerful. Surely, you think, he must be important.

"Kavalgyth!" you shout into the air. "Kavalgyth is the master."

The voice answers immediately, booming down in disappointed tones:

KAVALGYTH CANNOT MASTER EVEN HIS OWN RAGE! HE COULD NEVER BE MASTER OF THE TOWER.

You scratch your head and sigh, thoroughly discouraged. "But–"

CHOOSE ANOTHER.

Oh man, you get another shot! Let's get it right this time...

If you *know* who the master of the tower is, use the chart below to add up all the letters in that word. When you have the total you can *GO TO THAT PAGE*

A = 1	F = 6	K = 11	P = 16	U = 21	Z = 26
B = 2	G = 7	L = 12	Q = 17	V = 22	Example:
C = 3	H = 8	M = 13	R = 18	W = 23	ANNA =
D = 4	I = 9	N = 14	S = 19	X = 24	1+14+14+1
E = 5	J = 10	O = 15	T = 20	Y = 25	= 30

If you still don't know who the master is, *TURN TO PAGE 60*

108

There isn't a lot of time for indecision. You've already been in the tower for quite a while.

"I guess we'll take this one," you say to Finnegan, pointing at the oak door. "As long as we're going up."

"Oh we're *always* going up," Finny smiles. You smile back politely without any idea of what that means.

The area beyond the door is another hallway. You travel it for a very long time before ending up in another chamber, this one filled wall-to-wall with dozens of mirrors.

The irregular shape of the room makes it almost impossible to navigate. You can see an exit, but getting to it takes a lot of caution, backtracking, and bumping into walls of silvered glass.

"Uh oh," Finnegan says. You notice he has his nose just about pressed against the surface of a mirror. "It happened again."

"What did?"

Finny smiles as he takes a step back. "I got better lookin'!"

You roll your eyes as he starts to laugh. All of a sudden, your reflection starts laughing with him...

But you're not.

Finnegan looks on, fascinated. Your reflection continues laughing, staring silently back at you. Eventually the other you in the mirror winks, turns, and walks away. You're left looking at nothing.

"Wh– what do you think that means?" you ask.

"Dunno," Finny says. "I've never seen anything like that before." He examines you closely. "Sure there's not two of you?"

You shift back and forth, then wave your arms around. Nothing happens. You're starting to get creeped out. Standing in front of a mirror without a reflection is bizarrely unnerving.

"Come on," Finnegan says, slapping you hard on the back. "Quit playing." Together, he and a thousand of his reflections turn and exit the room.

Yeah man, quit playing!

Feel your way over to the exit *BY TURNING TO PAGE 138*

109

YON looks on with interest as you pull out your silver key. Grasping it by the elaborate octopus-sculpted head, you carefully insert it into the lock. It fits perfectly.

CLICK!

The glimmering silver gate swings wide. It opens into a grass-covered, circular area filled with fragrant smells and peaceful sounds. The light is warm. Everything here is exceptionally beautiful. It relaxes you, but in the back of your mind you know there's no time to enjoy it.

"What is this place?" you ask YON. But he doesn't answer.

In the center of the garden-like chamber is a pedestal carved in the form of flowing water. Atop it rests a gorgeously-crafted crystal snow globe. You pick it up and shake it. The scene inside looks like a winter version of the garden you're standing in, only now it's swirling with snow.

"And this?" you ask YON, holding up the snow globe. Again he says nothing. You tuck the snow globe in your pocket.

"For a guide you're not all that helpful YON," you tell him. "You know that?"

YON shifts. "*There was no one to help me when I was first banished here.*" Again, the voice in your head is laden with scorn and resentment. "*Like you, I had questions without answers. No one came to my aid.*"

You storm past him on the way back to the iron gate.

"Yeah, well way to pay it forward."

C'mon, YON can't be *all* bad, can he? Take the iron gate *BACK ON PAGE 14*

110

The card with the eye on it intrigues you. You feel... drawn to it.

Reaching down, you pick it up. There's a loud click, and a hidden door opens in the middle of the right-hand wall.

"Good enough!" Finny says. "And much better than last time."

"Last time?"

Finnegan grimaces and suppresses a shudder. He heads toward the exit.

"But–"

"You're in a hurry right?"

"Yeah."

Finnegan gestures you flamboyantly through the open door. "Then let's go!"

You getting tired of hurrying yet? Well too bad! *TURN TO PAGE 134*

111

The closer the mist gets, the more it spooks you. Eager to get out of it, you head for the clearing.

The ground here changes. It goes from snow to hard-packed dirt to a spongy, grass-like undergrowth. But what's even more fascinating is the sky. It seems to have come to life in colors you've never seen – stunning pinks and violets so stark and vibrant they appear almost painted on.

You're so wrapped up in watching the sky, you almost walk into the mist again. That's when another tremor hits, sundering the ground beneath you.

The earth opens. A rift appears as the ground continues to shake, spurring you to action. You run alongside the ever-growing fissure, determined not to be trapped on the wrong side of the clearing. It's a struggle to keep up as it continues tearing the ground ahead of you in a jagged, zig-zag pattern.

Eventually you win the race. You cross over to the other side of the clearing just as the mist swallows the area where you'd previously been standing. As you break free into a smaller area, the ground finally stops shaking. You rest your hands on your knees to catch your breath.

Directly in front of you, a smooth, cobbled path now cuts its way through the mist. Slightly off to one side of the path is something else: a rickety old rope bridge stretching across another, smaller chasm.

Once again, both choices seem to lead in the general direction you need to go.

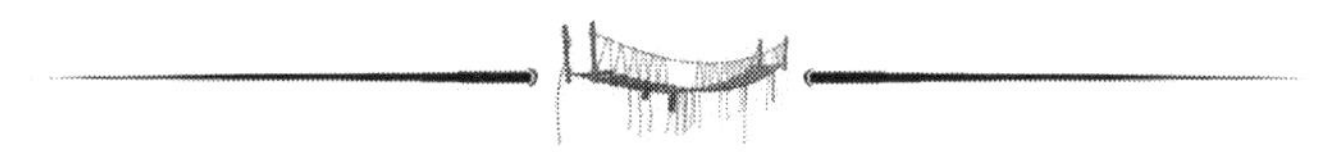

You can continue along the path when you *FLIP TO PAGE 33*

Or maybe the rickety rope bridge sounds better (really?) to you. If so, *TURN TO PAGE 63*

112

The latest staircase climbs in a tight spiral. Finnegan goes first, leading you higher and higher into the tower. Several minutes later, your legs are burning. You're also thirsty.

"Ah, we're here!" Finny says at last. He thrusts a glass of cold water your way. You have no idea where he got a glass of water, much less a cold one. You're too tired to ask.

The room is tiny – barely big enough for two people. A study iron ladder climbs up one wall, disappearing into the ceiling.

"More climbing?" you groan.

"For you, yes. Not for me."

You swallow the last gulp. Not only do you feel refreshed, you're almost like new again. "Let me guess," you say. "I'm on my own from here, right?"

"Always knew you were smart," Finnegan winks. He glances down at his watch. "Hey, one-thirty! We made good time!"

You frown. "How can is still be–"

Finny shrugs. "Trust me, it is."

"Maybe your watch is broken," you offer.

"Hmm," your friend tilts his head. "Never considered that." He holds it to his ear and shrugs. "Or maybe it's the tower that's broken?"

You hand the glass back to him and place one foot on the ladder. When you look up, it's nothing but rungs as far as the eye can see.

"Well, I hope you eventually get your hands on the guy running this place," Finny tells you.

"Uh, thanks. I'm sure I will."

"Me too," Finnegan says, looking you up and down with a smirk. He slaps you hard on the back. "Hey, you're alright! You know that?"

"Yeah," you say, wincing. "I do now..."

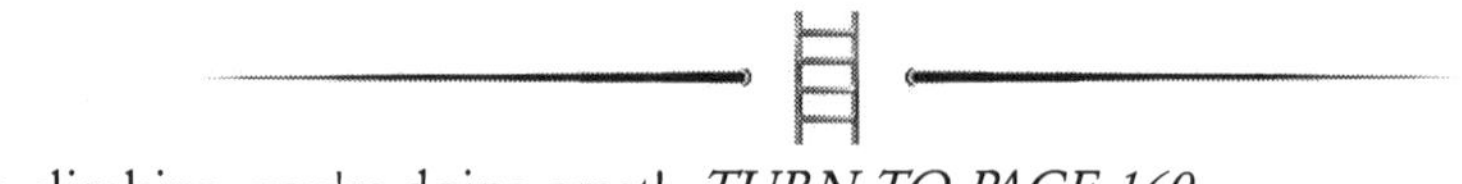

Keep climbing, you're doing great! *TURN TO PAGE 160*

113

The hallway slopes up, dragging you ever higher into the tower's topmost chambers. All this hard climbing is finally getting to you. Total exhaustion is not far off.

Up ahead, a small room ends in a single black door. YON stands there watching you. Waiting.

"I guess this is the way?" you sigh. You don't expect an answer. You don't get one.

Stepping up, you close your hand over the knob. It won't budge. You begin looking for a lock or keyhole, and that's when you notice a low hissing sound.

A fine pink mist starts rolling into the room. You have no clue where it's coming from. Instinctively you cover your mouth, trying not to breathe it in. But that's soon going to be impossible if you don't get the door open...

Quick! What color is YON?

If YON is RED, because you chose the red orb earlier, *TURN TO PAGE 86*

If YON is GOLD, because you chose the gold orb earlier, *GO TO PAGE 23*

114

"Thank you anyway," you tell Kara, "but I think Una's right." You hand her back the peach leaves. "I seem to remember something about planting mint to keep wasps and hornets away."

You crush the sprig of mint in your palms, rolling it back and forth to break up it. Then you rub it all over your hands and arms. You even do your neck for good measure. It smells... well, minty.

"Ready?" you ask. Kara nods in anticipation. Una looks a lot less sure. "Here goes!"

Carefully you approach the buzzing nest. The hornets don't seem to notice you, or change direction. You have to stand on you toes to reach it, but by moving with extreme slowness you're able to extract the object from the hive. There's a scary moment as the paper nest tears slightly, but you don't get stung!

You return to the sisters holding your prize. It's the figurine of a ballerina, masterfully carved out of a solid piece of ivory. Whoever crafted the object took painstaking care to make it as realistic as possible. It looks almost like a real person.

"She's beautiful!" Kara cries, clapping her hands. Since you really have no use for an ivory ballerina, you smile warmly and offer it to her.

"Oh no," Kara shakes her head. "She's yours. You need her."

"I what?"

"Come on," Una says, pulling her sister along the path. "Unlike you, he doesn't have all day."

Slip the ivory figurine into your pocket and *TURN TO PAGE 151*

115

All the letters you received said 'come alone'. Well, this voice is telling you to come. And right now, you're certainly alone.

You take another step forward. Then another. Finally realizing you could no longer resist if you wanted to, you give in and succumb to the forces drawing you in.

Light floods you, orange and warm. It goes through you. Into you. And with the light comes knowledge.

This is the core. The source of all power.

In your mind's eye you see it all. The tower... its purpose... every corridor, every hallway, every mortared stone and hidden secret. You know nothing. You know everything.

You *are* everything.

A booming laugh echoes across the basement, all menacing and hollow. The laughter is a chorus of a thousand voices. One of them is your own.

This *is* the power source for the Tower of Never There. Congratulations. You are now one of the batteries.

For the being you've just become, this is a new beginning. But for the person formerly known as Tyler Paulsen, this is unequivocally

---

THE END

116

The staircase winds upward for several minutes before finally ending in a stone chamber. There are no exits, no doors – the room is completely empty except for a small table.

"Oh," Finny says. "This again."

Spread out on the surface of the table are four cards. As you get closer you can see they're covered with colorful, mesmerizing artwork.

"These look like Tarot cards," you say. You have vague recollections of your favorite aunt doing readings with you as a child. It's a memory that makes you smile.

For the first time, Finnegan looks apprehensive. "Sort of," he says.

The four cards are very different. One is of a serpent. Another of a very wide, surprised-looking eye. There's also the unmistakable form of the grim reaper hunched over his scythe, and a card depicting a shadowy figure kneeling in the rain.

"What do you mean, sort of?"

"Well, you're going to have to pick one," Finny continues.

You blink. "Me? Pick one?"

Finnegan nods. "Yes. Or we can't go on."

117

Looks like you're stuck with picking a card. Better choose wisely!

To pick the card with the REAPER on it, *HEAD TO PAGE 175*

To pick the card with the SNAKE on it, *TURN TO PAGE 162*

To pick the card with the EYE on it, *FLIP TO PAGE 110*

To pick the card with the SHADOWY FIGURE on it, *GO TO PAGE 46*

118

You walk over, pick up the red orb, and place it on the stand. Almost immediately the strange being shifts colors. Its thousands of tiny lights change from shimmering, glimmering silver to a deep, blood red.

"*I am YON,*" the creature speaks. It has no face, no eyes, no mouth. In fact, the voice you hear is somehow coming from inside your own head. "*I know what it is that you seek.*" With that, the light-being exits the chamber. "*Come. There is little time.*"

Spurred on by the creature's sense of urgency, you follow it through a series of narrow hallways. At first you say nothing, but the silence soon becomes awkward.

"Thank you YON," you say as you catch up to the creature. It nods once briefly, its lights flashing pink as it hurries along. "I appreciate the help."

"*I am obligated to help,*" YON replies. "*Nothing less, nothing more.*" Though he speaks only in your mind, you detect an obvious bitterness in the creature's voice.

"So you're trapped here too?"

YON flashes a violet color. He stops walking. "*Exiled,*" he says finally. "*By my own people.*"

"Why?"

The creature of light begins moving again, this time even more quickly. If he says something else you don't hear him.

119

Eventually the hallway opens into a much wider area. Paintings line the walls in golden gilt frames. You see sculptures, tapestries, and other collections of beautiful artwork arranged in various displays. The place is unmistakably some sort of museum.

"What is all this stuff?" you ask. "And who put it here?"

YON says nothing as you pass through the gallery. Many of the sculptures are of creatures you've never seen. The paintings, when you examine them, depict strange, foreign landscapes. You're leaning in for a closer look when, all of a sudden, you feel the floor shift beneath you.

"*Get down!*" YON shouts in your head.

The rumble turns into a tremor, and the entire tower shakes. A block of stone breaks off somewhere overhead. You can sense it at the edges of your peripheral vision, screaming down at you...

"*Move, quickly! Starboar- I mean, to your side!*"

You have less than half a second to dive out of harms way! Quick - Which direction do you go?

To dive to your left, *TURN TO PAGE 106*

To dive to your right, *HEAD TO PAGE 125*

120

The button with the fountain seems innocent enough. You press it.

Right away something happens. There's a hollow boom from within one of the walls, and a door opens behind you.

You move inside to find a small, empty chamber. A quick search reveals nothing. There are no exits, no other entrances – only the way you came in. But when you turn around to leave, YON is standing in the doorway...

Pop quiz, hotshot! When you first met YON, did you turn him RED or GOLD?

If you chose the RED orb when you first encountered YON, *GO TO PAGE 64*

If you chose the GOLD orb when you first met YON, *TURN TO PAGE 19*

121

You pull out the lotus blossom Kara gave you. Like the dancer, it's overwhelmingly beautiful.

Holding it up, you offer it to her...

But the ballerina pays no attention. She spins into your hand, knocking the flower to the ground!

She's still whirling. Faster and faster...

Quick! Try something else...

If you have the Jeweled Pin you can offer that instead *ON PAGE 173*
If you have the Bone Horn, try blowing it *OVER ON PAGE 67*
If you have the Snow Globe, shake it up and *FLIP TO PAGE 24*

If you have none of these items, *TURN TO PAGE 137*

122

You draw the carved soldier figure from your pocket. Placing it on the smooth ebony pedestal, you step back.

Shadows form. The room dissolves into near darkness. A chill wind picks up, and the smell of earth and smoke reaches your nostrils.

When you look down the stone floor has changed to hard-packed dirt! You're somewhere else. Maybe. Maybe not.

There's the clink of metal. The scent of oil and steel. You whirl, trying to pick up the source of the noise, and that's when the soldier steps into view.

The man's features are obscured by shadow, but you can see that he's helmeted. The man is tall. Strong. In one hand he holds a steel-grey broadsword, while strapped to the other is a rounded shield.

"Uh... hey," you call out.

The soldier bangs his shield with his sword and begins advancing toward you.

"Whoa! Hold on! Wait a minute!"

He swings! You jump back. The blade slices through the air with a loud *whoosh!*

"Can we talk about this?"

You're pretty sure the first attack was meant as a warning. Maybe a warm-up. Now however, the soldier is really closing the distance. He's coming on fast!

You'd better do something...

There's not much time! Do you have anything that will get you out of this?

If you own the Lotus Blossom you can offer it to the soldier *ON PAGE 32*

If you own the Jeweled Pin you can try giving him that instead *ON PAGE 98*

If you own the Bone Horn maybe now is a good time to blow it? If this is your choice, *HEAD TO PAGE 51*

If you own the Snow Globe you can also try shaking things up. You can make that happen by *GOING TO PAGE 144*

If you have none of these things, *FLIP TO PAGE 168*

123

You fly into the tower at full speed, sprinting past a pair of young, waifish women with dark curly hair. The interior is well-lit, warm and dry. One of the girls closes the door behind you.

"Welcome!" she says excitedly. "And nice running!"

You stop to catch your breath. The inside of the tower is enormous! The ceiling – if you could call it that – is hundreds of feet overhead. Left to right, wall to wall, you see nothing but plants and trees and breathtaking gardens. Everything is impossibly huge! As if the tower were somehow bigger on the inside than it is on the outside.

"What are you doing here?" the other girl asks. "It's not often we get visitors!"

You turn to face them for the first time. Both girls are identical, from their lovely olive skin to their thick, bouncy hair. It's obvious they're not only sisters, they're twins! The only difference is that one has the most amazing green eyes, while the other has eyes that are ice blue.

"My name is Una," the green-eyed girl says. "This is my sister, Kara."

Kara curtsies and smiles at you warmly. "So uh, what's your name?"

"Tyler," you say, still a little bit out of breath. "I'm Tyler. And, wow... what *is* this place?"

Una and Kara glance at each other. "Well, we're not *entirely* sure," Kara answers. "But we call it the Tower of Never There."

"Never there?"

They nod in unison. "That's because, well, it's not always here," says Una.

"Or there, really," Kara adds.

You have no idea what they're talking about... nothing they're saying makes any sense! The sisters seem to sense your confusion.

"The tower moves," Una says. "It blinks."

"Blinks?" You blink.

"Yup," Kara affirms. "Every hour, on the hour." Her expression grows sad. "It used to be different. But not anymore."

Your gaze is drawn upward, to the cavernous, indoor garden. A colorful bird zips by. The smell of lilacs wafts past your nostrils. You can hear what sounds like a waterfall somewhere off in the distance.

"So where does it go?" you ask. "The tower?"

"All different places," Una says.

"All different *times*," Kara chimes in. Her sister gives her what might be considered a dirty look. Kara shrugs.

124

You regard the twins carefully. They don't appear to be deceiving you, at least intentionally. Still, your eyes narrow.

"So you're saying I'm in a teleporting, time-traveling tower," you begin, "and that in less than an hour I'll be somewhere else?"

"We," Una corrects you. "*We'll* be somewhere else."

"Or some *time* else." Kara says. Preemptively, she sticks her tongue out at her sister.

Every hour, on the hour... You glance back at the massive twin doors. The sisters follow your gaze.

"Oh, you can't leave," one of them tells you. "Not now. Not until the tower is done with you."

"Done with me?" You scratch behind your ear. "I don't even know what I'm doing here!"

The girls look thoroughly confused. "Then why'd you even come?" asks Una.

Hastily you pull out the latest envelope and unfold the parchment. The twins read the letter with great interest. A strange look passes between them.

"Well there's only one way to figure this out for sure," Kara says. "You need to go up."

"Up?"

"Yes, up. To see the boss."

You shake your head, as if to clear it. The motion only makes you dizzy. "The boss, huh?" The idea, you suppose, isn't all that crazy. In fact, right about now you'd love to talk to the person in charge. "And how do we go up?" you ask.

"You," Una says. "*You* go up. But we can still help you," she adds cheerfully. "Follow us." With that, the girls bound down a pretty stone path that winds its way through the garden.

Kara smiles at you over her shoulder. She looks you up and down for a second, and then pauses. "Hey, you forgot your backpack."

"My backpa–"

"Never mind her," Una tells you. "Come."

I guess you'd better come. *TURN TO PAGE 53*

125

Starboar–

There's no time to think! You dive to the right... just as a half-ton block of stone whizzes past your leg! It shatters into a thousand pieces right were you were standing, obliterating the tiled floor and scattering chunks of jagged rock in all directions.

You pick yourself up and turn to face YON. "Starboard?"

"*My apologies for the confusion,*" YON says. "*Though I speak your language, my dialect is imperfect. The nautical term came to me because I am...*" he pauses here to correct himself, "*I* was once *a great navigator of the stars.*"

"Well you saved my life!" you say. "Thank you!"

YON pauses for a second, then nods. On impulse you move to hug him. As you do, your entire body is flung backwards with a giant electric shock!

"*You should not touch me,*" YON advises. "*I am not... like you.*"

Rising again more slowly, you dust yourself off for the second time. Your whole body tingles. "Yes, well... um, thanks again. I owe you one."

But the crimson being shakes its head. "*I am owed nothing.*" A small aftershock rumbles through the room, sending down another shower of dust. "*Come, we must hurry. We have delayed too long.*"

Well, what are you waiting for? *TURN TO PAGE 170*

126

"I can't choose," you tell YON. "I have nothing to put on any of the pedestals."

Your light-friend flashes, then dims. He looks you up and down.

"*Nothing?*"

You shake your head. "Sorry."

YON's entire demeanor changes. Up until this moment you'd detected a rising sense of excitement. But now, the being of light only seems... dejected.

"*Then you cannot proceed.*"

A sudden anger seizes you. "What do you mean I can't proceed? I came all this way! I did everything I was supposed to–"

"*There's nothing I can–*"

Without warning, light flares. This time it enters through the windows, coming from outside the tower. It grows brighter and brighter, until you're shielding your eyes from it. Which is impossible, of course, because it's night.

"What in the world–"

A wooziness washes over you, followed by a complete loss of equilibrium. Head spinning, you're dropped to your knees. Everything shakes. No, shakes isn't exactly the right word. Everything *shifts*.

"YON!"

127

You can't move. You can't even breathe. Then there's an explosion of light, and in that a split second it feels like your brain blossoms outward, separating into billions of tiny pieces that are just as quickly forced back together again. Like some sort of giant jigsaw puzzle...

A jigsaw puzzle of *yourself.*

Then, once again, you're standing. The world is still spinning as you clutch your head. The whole chamber appears different. The light is gone!

Outside, the landscape has changed. Dark rolling seas dominate every direction, broken only by tiny islands of jagged rock. Large winged creatures swoop in lazy circles high overhead, bigger – and stranger – than anything you've ever seen.

"The tower..."

"*Blinked,*" YON finishes for you. "*Yes.*"

You stare down at the floor. There's a lump in your throat.

"*For what it is worth,*" YON continues, "*I am sorry.*"

Well, you came close. Oh so close! At least now you'll get to see strange new things, new lands, new people. Heck, maybe Finnegan will even show you around!

That adventure is just beginning. But I'm afraid your time trying to solve the mystery of the tower has reached

---

THE END

128

Backing up slowly, you pull out the crystal snow globe. Maybe it does something. Heck, maybe it has magical powers! That wouldn't be so hard to believe, right? After all, you *are* staring at a dragon!

With a firm grip on the globe, you shake it violently. Glitter swirls through the tiny interior landscape, creating the world's smallest blizzard. The dragon squints one eye, watching you curiously.

It doesn't look impressed.

Well, I suppose it was worth a shot. Drop the snow globe and try something else:

If you have the Lotus Blossom, you can give it to the dragon instead by *TURNING TO PAGE 177*

If you have the Jeweled Pin, that's another option. Try that one *OVER ON PAGE 81*

If you have the Bone Horn, you can try to sound it. Put it to your lips and *GO TO PAGE 161*

Finally, think back to the indoor garden. Did you pet the Saspernink? If so, *FLIP TO PAGE 136*

If you obtained or accomplished none of these things, *TURN TO PAGE 68*

129

The angel swoops low, chittering through her broken grin. You counter by pulling out the lotus blossom Kara gave you and holding it up to her.

SWAT!

When you look up again your hand is empty. The angel has batted the flower away. Her wings flap noisily as she enters a climbing turn, getting ready to drop down on you again. She's still grinning.

Well, that didn't work! What do you do now?

If you have the Jeweled Pin, try giving her that *OVER ON PAGE 87*

If you have the Bone Horn, sound it loudly and *GO TO PAGE 31*

If you have the Snow Globe, try shaking it vigorously and *HEAD TO PAGE 43*

If you have none of these items, *FLIP DOWN TO PAGE 178*

130

You forgot your backpack, your knife, your canteen... it's all sitting there back at the campsite, just up the ridge. It's really not that far at all.

Turning around, you face the mist. Maybe it's not as thick as it looks. Maybe it'll even thin out as you climb the hill again, and you'll be able to retrieve your equipment. Might as well try.

Holding your breath, you stride purposefully into the fog. Instantly you regret the decision. You can't see your hand in front of your face, and only seconds later, your eyes begin to sting. Since you're already blind you squeeze them shut, but tears are now streaming down your face. They touch your lips and taste like acid.

You trip. Maybe on a root, or maybe on something else. In the strange fog, it's impossible to know. As you strike the ground it knocks the wind from you. You breathe in and are wracked by a terrible, involuntary fit of coughing.

The mist, or fog, or whatever it is – it's poison!

Luckily you still have your sense of direction. You scramble backward on all fours and make your way out of the brume. Coughing the last of the putrid fog from your lungs, you're thrilled to finally take a deep, sweet breath of clean mountain air!

As you wipe the tears from your eyes you glance back on the only two choices still left to you.

You can head into the open, mist-free clearing *OVER ON PAGE 111*
Or you can check out the ancient, gnarled tree *BY TURNING TO PAGE 44*

131

Alright, you figure. If Finny wants this guy taken down, there has to be a good reason for it. Besides, this is the 'big guy'. And hasn't it been your goal all along to find the boss of the tower?

Creeping along as silently as possible, you make your way over to Finnegan. He motions you past him, and soon you're standing beside the ledge.

"What do we do now?" you whisper back.

Finnegan answers by holding his hands out like claws. Silently he mimes a springing motion.

You peek around the corner of the wall. The man still has his back to you. He's not big, not small – about your size, really. You could probably take him.

"Do it now!" Finnegan hisses. He shoos you forward with both hands.

Thinking ninja thoughts, you crouch down and creep forward. As you do, your target moves as well. He must hear you!

You spring quickly, before you lose him. Only your opponent leaps forward just as fast. You find yourself off balance, sprawling across the ledge. Your heart catches in your throat as you realize how high you are above the ground!

Roll two dice! (Or just pick a random number from 2 to 12)

If you roll an 8 or under, *GO TO PAGE 92*

If you roll a 9 or over, *SKIP DOWN TO PAGE 176*

132

"I... I don't know what to do!" you shout. The snake is nearly upon you.

"Quick," Finnegan says. "In here!"

Your friend has thrown open a door. Which makes no sense, because just a minute ago there wasn't a single door leading out of the room.

With the serpent bearing down on you, you allow Finnegan to push you through the door. He follows you in and slams it closed, blanketing you in total darkness.

"Uh oh. Darn. This room again."

You don't like that sound of any of that. "Darn? What room?"

"This one," Finny replies, as if the answer is as plain as day. "The one with the disappearing door."

"Disappearing *door?*" You reach past him in the darkness, feeling for the opening you just came through. Sure enough the wall is smooth. There's nothing there.

"Yeah," Finny says apologetically. "The last time this happened I was stuck in here for two days."

"TWO DAYS?"

"Yes, but don't worry," he says hurriedly. "It'll go fast. I've got *tons* of great stories to help pass the time."

You place your back against the wall and sink slowly to the floor. *Two days!*

"Wanna hear some good ones?" Finny asks merrily. "Well once, back when I was downstairs..."

Yikes. Looks like you're in for a treat! At least you'll be out eventually. Whether or not you'll maintain your sanity is another issue.

For now, you've arrived at

THE END

133

You find the path again, and are moving along nicely when something else happens:

It begins to rain.

"Seriously?" you ask. You try to look up but only succeed in getting water in your eyes. "It's raining *inside* the tower?"

Kara is laughing at you. Una actually manages a smirk too.

"Don't you think that's a little strange?" you say in exasperation.

Una shakes her head. "You haven't been here long," she says, "but you've been here long enough to realize that *nothing* is considered strange in this place." As if to illustrate her point the rain comes down even harder. "Come," Una says. "Stand over here."

You follow the sisters to a dry area – a thick canopy of trees not far from the path. The rain has a strange, coppery smell to it. You look down at your watch and immediately realize you don't have a watch.

"It'll pass quickly," Una assures you. "It always does."

She's right. A minute or two later, the rain is no more than a drizzle. You feel a tap on your shoulder. It's Kara.

"Look."

A bit deeper into the trees, where the forest grows darker, you see a series of thick white spiderwebs. They criss-cross the entire area. They're also the biggest webs you've ever seen.

"Glad we don't have to go that wa–"

"No," Kara interjects. "Look there." She points. Spun into one of the webs you can see a beautiful silver key. It protrudes in your direction.

"It's so pretty!" Kara gasps. "You should get that!"

"No," says Una. "You shouldn't."

Do you extract the silver key from the spiderweb? Try it *BACK ON PAGE 96*

Or would you rather not mess with giant spiders? Skip it and *GO TO PAGE 148*

134

The hall ends in a spacious, high-ceilinged room with a terraced floor. It's filled on every level with glass tanks and containers of all shapes and sizes.

"The collection room," Finny announces. "Cool, huh?"

You can't help but stare at all the colorful aquariums and terrariums. Many of the specimens within are fish and creatures you recognize. But some you absolutely do not.

"Where does all this stuff come from?"

"Well," Finnegan begins, "the tower travels. You know that already. So as it moves from place to place, it sometimes picks things up." He points and laughs. "Like you, for example."

You smirk back at him. "And you too, pal."

Finnegan laughs. "True enough."

"So it's like a big sticky ball," you offer, "rolling through time and space, picking things up as it cruises along?"

"YES!" Finnegan cries. He claps his hands together gleefully. "Yes! That's a *fantastic* way of putting it!"

Your friend never stops moving. He leads you rapidly through the room, weaving his way between tall rows of fascinating-looking containers. Eventually, something catches your eye.

"What's this?" You're pointing to a beautiful-looking beetle that shimmers in all different metallic colors. Also in its tank you notice a handful of what appear to be raw, uncut gemstones.

"Oh that's a Mymerrian," Finnegan says casually. "Pretty, isn't it?"

"But aren't those..."

"Gems? Yes, they are. Very high quality, in fact."

You swallow hard. "Does it eat them?"

"Oh no," Finnegan says. He suddenly looks uncomfortable. "In fact, err... just the opposite." He blushes and shrugs. "The Mymerrian is a carnivore. It eats other animals."

"You mean other insects," you correct him.

"No," Finnegan says. "I mean other *animals*."

135

You examine the beetle more carefully. You see no stingers, no barbs, not even evidence of any pincers.

"This thing can't be dangerous."

"It is," Finny assures you from over his shoulder.

It's not long before your gaze shifts back to the gemstones. The tank isn't all that deep. You could easily reach into it. And the uncut rocks are huge! They look like they could be rubies, sapphires, emeralds...

"Uh, I'd be careful bud," Finnegan warns. You wonder if he's reading your mind. "That thing hasn't been fed in quite a while."

The tank is shallow, the beetle small. The jewels are easily within reach! Then again...

Do you swipe the uncut gemstones from the terrarium? If so *GO TO PAGE 88*

Or would you rather just leave well enough alone? Leave the collection room through the exit hallway and *GO TO PAGE 138*

136

The dragon glares down at you disdainfully. There's no place to run. Nowhere to hide. It stretches its head to come face to face with you, and its lips curl back in a hideous grin.

There must be something you can do! But before anything comes to mind the creature snorts... then sneezes!

A loathsome mixture of heat, moisture, and noxious gases washes over you. Bile fills your throat as your eyes turn to water. You're seconds away from gagging! Reflexively you put your arm up...

...and the dragon stops.

You hold your breath as you watch it. It sniffs the air once, twice, then rears back in utter disgust!

You stare down at your hand, and that's when you realize it: *The Saspernink!*

Your whole hand still smells like the powerful musk released by the loud, fiery creature. And it's a good thing it does, because it looks like the dragon is allergic!

The dragon sneezes again. Twice, then three more times. It rears back, slinks into the shadows, and disappears.

Before your eyes the darkness fades... and you're right back in the pedestal chamber. The walls, the floor – everything materializes back into view, becoming solid and corporeal again.

"*You were lucky,*" YON's voice echoes. He's standing beside you.

"Sometimes luck is all you need," you tell him.

The light-being points. In the center of the room a platform is rising slowly up from the floor. He indicates that you should be on it.

You'd better hurry.

Leap up onto the platform and *FLIP BACK TO PAGE 100*

137

The crazy ballerina is still coming... but you have nothing to fend her off with!

Moving quickly, you side-step. The dancer whirls past you, turns, and adjusts her trajectory again. No matter how much you try to avoid her, she just keeps coming. It's like she has it out for you!

"Stop!"

You try calling out to her, but there's no response. No change in her behavior. She crashes toward you again. Once more you spin out of the way.

There's a humming sound. A thrumming. It's coming from beneath you. A vibration that feels like it did when you were back in the clearing...

The tower!

Suddenly you look up. You forgot all about the ballerina!

WHAM!

You wake up dizzy and light-headed. Light streams in from the windows of the upper chamber. The dancer is gone. So is YON. But outside, you can see everything else is radically different...

Hesitantly you edge your way over to one of the window panes. The original landscape is gone. There's nothing now but ocean and whitecaps and strange rock formations that form little islands all around you. Even the color of the water is all wrong.

The tower blinked.

The knowledge is crushing. You have no way home.

Nothing to do now but accept that this is

THE END

138

The corridor you're taking ends in a vast, reaching chamber. It's bisected down the middle by a long, seemingly bottomless chasm.

You want to ask Finnegan how the enormity of such a place could exist in here, or why there would be a chasm inside of a tower in the first place. But there simply isn't time. Instead, you keep your questions more practical.

"How do we get across?"

Your friend points. Spanning the chasm is a stone formation that looks, impossibly, like a natural rock bridge.

"The bridge is in today!" Finny cries. "Good thing, too."

As you make your approach the span appears uncomfortably narrow. It looks less like a bridge and more like a catwalk. "This thing safe?" you ask.

Finnegan scrambles up the stone arch in answer. He reaches the center of the bridge and stops to wait for you.

You start across. The bridge is not only sturdy, the footing is good too. But as you reach Finnegan, and the halfway point, you make the mistake of looking down. In just seconds you're mesmerized by the swirling, inky darkness.

"What's down there?"

"Dunno," he says, "never jumped." Finnegan looks thoughtful, then suddenly excited. He grabs your wrist and looks down. "Should we?"

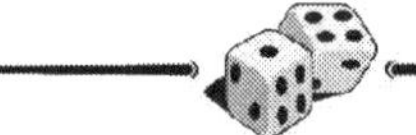

If you grin deviously back at Finny and jump, roll two dice! (Or just pick a random number from 2 to 12)

If you roll a 3, 4, 9 or 11, *FLY ON DOWN TO PAGE 77*

If you roll anything else, *DROP QUICKLY BACK TO PAGE 48*

If you think jumping into the swirling darkness of a bottomless chasm is absolutely crazy, you haven't been hanging out with Finnegan long enough. Continue across the bridge and *TURN TO PAGE 66*

139

The lightning is everywhere! The thunder is deafening! It's just too much!

Turning back, you sprint for the cover of the large tree. The canopy shelters you from the rain. You hug your body tightly against the large trunk...

Wait a minute, you think to yourself. A disquieting thought enters your head. *Aren't trees* dangerous *in a lightning storm?*

KA-RAAACK!

Oops. Looks like this might be

THE END

140

The pole slides into hole number three. There's a hollow tearing sound, as if something's been pierced, and then an object falls down from the ceiling.

Finnegan picks it up and looks it over. "It's a horn."

You blink. "What kind of horn?"

"See for yourself." He hands it to you. It's a beautifully carved horn of bone. A hunting, or maybe a battle horn. You run your fingers over the rawhide thong.

"Whose is this?"

"It's yours now boss," Finnegan says. "That's how it works."

You scratch behind your ear. "Don't you think that's strange?"

"Strange?" Finnegan laughs. "I find all sorts of stuff here." He fishes around in his pocket for a moment and a half-dozen small objects fall to the floor. You see gum balls, dice, a mostly-eaten candy bar. Reaching down, you pick up a small brass plate with four tiny screws.

"What's this?" you ask.

"Got it off the door of a hotel room I once stayed at," Finny says. "Real weird place, even for me!"

You shake your head and hand it back to him.

"Come on," Finnegan says, throwing open the door. We need to keep going."

Sling your new horn over your shoulder and *HEAD BACK TO PAGE 66*

141

"It must spell DANGER," you reason. "Look at the position of the letters. DANGER fits perfectly."

Kara looks at her sister. Una scratches her chin. "What about the extra letter?" she asks. "The second 'E'?"

You shrug. "Maybe they had leftovers," you reason. "You know, from the last time they changed the sign." Truthfully, you really have no clue. You're still struggling with the concept of indoor gardens and teleporting towers.

"Alright then," Kara says. "If the left path is dangerous, we take the right fork!"

The two of them skip along before you can say another word. You follow quickly, throwing one last look back to the broken sign. Maybe the extra letter *did* mean something. Then again, maybe it didn't.

Eventually, the path widens out. It becomes lined on both sides with some of the strangest-looking but most beautiful trees you've ever seen. Some grow in colors you didn't realize trees could even come in. Like blue, for example.

"Hey, wait up," you say as the sisters get uncomfortably far ahead of you. "What's this–"

"Ohhh!" Kara suddenly cries. "Look at that!"

You catch up. Dangling from a vine on one of the strange trees is a rainbow-colored orchid. The blossom actually shimmers and changes as you look at it from different angles. It's the most incredible flower you've ever seen.

"I want that!" Kara gasps. She turns her ice blue eyes on you. "Please?"

Una looks uncertain. "Umm... I don't know about that..."

The flower hangs a good deal off the ground. You're the only one who can reach it.

If you choose *not* to reach up and pick the flower, that's fine (crush a girl's dreams why don't you?) Continue on down the stone path *OVER ON PAGE 30*

If you *do* pick the flower for Kara, roll two dice (or just pick a random number from 2 to 12)

If the roll comes up an ODD number, *HEAD TO PAGE 93*

If the roll comes up an EVEN number, *FLIP BACK TO PAGE 11*

142

You remember the moss-covered boulder, and the riddle carved into it. Una and Kara watch you closely.

"Back to move forward," you say with a shrug. As bizarre as it seems, you turn around and begin walking backwards.

Una smiles and places her hands on your shoulders. "And down to go up," she adds. With that, she guides you in the direction of the basement steps.

It goes against every instinct you have, but you walk down the basement steps. Backwards. Into the darkness. Only a few steps down you're overwhelmed with a strange vertigo. You feel lightheaded. Dizzy. Like you're about to fall...

When you come to, you're standing on a tiny ramp more than a hundred feet in the air! The indoor garden is spread out far beneath you, shrouded in mist. All you can see are birds zipping by, and the tops of a few trees poking through.

"The mirror of reason fills chaos's cup," a voice says merrily. You turn and see Kara. She and her sister are somehow standing beside you.

"Was... was this the chaos then?" you ask. You're still woozy. Looking down makes your legs feel weak.

"Not even close," Una laughs.

There's a small, square-shaped door in the wall behind you. It's already open. "Is that where we go next?" you ask.

"Not we," Kara says. "*You.*"

Una nods. "You'll have to go on without us from here," she affirms. "We cannot go further."

The sisters smile, and each of them gives you a great big hug. Kara's hug goes on extra long.

"It was nice meeting you a–"

Her sentence is never finished. Una yanks her sister forcibly backward, and together they go over the edge!

Expecting the worst, you drop to your knees and peer out over the lip of the platform. To your shock the twins are okay! Somehow they're floating, rather than falling.

"Goodbyeeee Tyler!' they call back in unison. "And good luck!" Holding hands, they slowly and gently disappear into the mist below.

Duck through the odd square door *WHEN YOU TURN TO PAGE 73*

143

The smoke overwhelms you. It obscures your vision, drags you to the floor...

You come to and find yourself somewhere else entirely. It's a room, but then again maybe it's not. Everything is white. The floor, walls, ceiling... it's all blindingly bright. You see nothing in every direction. Nothing except the mirror on the opposite end.

Slowly you stand. You don't feel tired anymore. There's no exhaustion, no stiffness in your legs from climbing all those stairs. You cross the room easily and stand before the mirror. Inside it you see yourself.

But *not* yourself.

A feeling comes over you. It's difficult to explain. You're certain you're no longer in the vision chamber, yet something familiar keeps pulling at the back of your mind.

You reach out with one hand. You touch the mirror...

... purple smoke engulfs you again.

Wake back up *OVER ON PAGE 163*

144

The soldier swings! This time you duck. Spinning to one side, you reach into your pocket and pull out the crystal snow globe.

You shake it. Hard. Tiny flecks of glittering snow swirl around the miniature landscape, which now looks beautiful, peaceful, and serene.

Whoosh!

The sword slices the air again, this time right beside your ear! Close call! You back up a few feet, just as the soldier is getting ready to charge with his shield.

The snow globe is obviously not helping. You drop it.

Well *that* didn't work. Got anything else in your bag of tricks?

If you own the Lotus Blossom, try handing that to the soldier *ON PAGE 32*

If you own the Jeweled Pin, maybe he wants that instead? *GO TO PAGE 98*

If you own the Bone Horn, take a deep breath and blow it. *TURN TO PAGE 51*

If you obtained none of these things, *FLIP TO PAGE 168*

145

Thinking feather-light thoughts, you set foot on the rope bridge. It creaks and groans even louder than you expected. Your fingers close in a death-grip over the frayed rope handholds, and as the bridge tilts one way you shift your weight in the opposite direction.

The wood isn't as rotten as it first looked. It's even *worse.* You're a quarter of the way across when the first of the slats break apart. For some reason you continue onward, trying not look down. But of course you *do* look down, and what you see freezes your blood cold.

You see sky.

The area beneath the bridge is a mirror image of the strange violet sky above you. A vivid recollection returns from your childhood; a memory of lying on your back, staring up at the endless sky, and wondering what it would be like to fall *up.* Wondering how it would feel if the Earth somehow released its hold on you, flinging you through the clouds...

Suddenly the bridge shakes. Or rather, the ground on either side of it is shaking. Rocks tumble down from the surrounding hillside. It's another earthquake!

Quick, roll a single die! (Or just pick a random number from 1 to 6)

If the number is a 3 or a 6, *TURN BACK TO PAGE 15*

If the number is a 1, 2, 4 or 5, *HEAD ON OVER TO PAGE 59*

146

You drop to the ground! There's the whistle of razor-sharp talons as the creature buzzes past one ear, then swoops high into the air and begins flying away. You watch it until it becomes nothing more than a dot against the weird purple sky.

Turning your attention back to the forest path you continue onward, moving deeper into the shadows. What seemed at first to be a small copse of trees has expanded into a thick, overgrown forest. In most places, light hardly penetrates the many layers of trees. You didn't see any of this from your campsite up on the mountain ridge, but now it seems like the forest canopy extends in every direction.

A few minutes later, you stop. You're starting to lose any sense of where you are. Is the tower still straight ahead? Suddenly you're not so sure. You turn in a slow circle, scanning the area, and that's when you notice the cave.

It's dark. The entrance is covered in moss. You take a few steps in its direction and hear a high-pitched chattering sound echoing from inside.

BOOM!

The new sound is loud. Hollow. But instead of coming from the cave, the source of the noise seems to be further down the path. You're not sure what to do, but you're starting to get antsy. The mist is a lot closer than it was before...

Well, you can't stay in the forest forever. So what's next?

If you investigate the booming noise along the forest path, *HEAD TO PAGE 102*

If you'd rather check out the cave instead, *GO TO PAGE 47*

147

The minotaur is just too fast! It scoops you up, holding you to dangle before it as easily as you might pick up a small child.

"Finnegan! Help!"

The creature roars directly into your face. Hot, putrid bull-breath washes over you in a nauseating wave. You're woozy... dizzy...

You come to and find yourself in a large iron cage, in another part of the tower. Kavalgyth is pacing back and forth nearby. He's grunting and snorting fiercely as he argues with Finnegan.

"I know, I know..." Finnegan says. "But it's not his fault. You cant–"

The bull-creature roars, blowing Finnegan's hair back from his face. Your friend lowers his shoulders dejectedly.

Cautiously you move to the edge of your cell. "Wh– what does he want?" you ask. You're standing there, gripping the bars.

Finny sighs. "Well the good news is I got you off easy. He's not going to eat you."

"He's not... *what?*" After the blood finishes draining from your face, you let out a long, relieved breath.

"The bad news is you're gonna be here a while," Finny continues. "Maybe a month. Not more than two."

The minotaur, who has been listening to all of this, grunts twice.

"Oh yeah," Finnegan adds, "and he wants to know if you can cook."

A MONTH OR TWO?

Your legs go limp as you allow yourself to sink to the cold stone floor. It would certainly seem that your adventure has reached

---

THE END

148

The garden path ends in a circular seating area, complete with tiled mosaic benches and a central marble fountain. There, a massive staircase winds itself in a spiral around the tower's inner wall.

"There you go," Una says, gesturing proudly. "Up."

Your breath catches in your throat. The staircase is steep and narrow. There's also no railing. You think about climbing it while trying desperately not to trip, hugging the wall, resisting the urge to look down. Your stomach drops.

"Wow. You should be careful," Kara says. And if *she's* advising caution, now you know you're *really* in trouble!

The base of the staircase, you notice, also continues downward. Stone steps descend steeply into the darkness beneath the tower.

"There's a basement too?" you ask incredulously.

"Sorta," answers Una. She looks a little unsure though. Maybe even slightly uncomfortable.

You glance reluctantly back at the long spiral of narrow steps that trail upward. They disappear into the gentle mist that rises from the garden. It's impossible to even see where they end.

"Will you climb it with me?" you ask without thinking. Immediately you feel foolish.

"Uh... sorta," says Kara.

Una delivers you a serious look. "So which way are you going, Tyler? Up or down?"

To start climbing that staircase, *GO TO PAGE 40*
If you'd rather descend, *HEAD TO PAGE 142*

149

You decide to stick to the wider cavern. But then it slopes down, and down, and down. Things get damp and dark, and the bats are still swirling around you. The air is also getting stale.

With your arms up to ward the creatures off, it's difficult to see. Not to mention how your phone's light flashes wildly around the cavern as you run.

A bat strikes your head... and latches onto your ear! Your hand shoots up to yank it off, but then your legs fall behind your body. You're off balance... pinwheeling forward... arms flailing wildly to regain your footing until–

WHAM!

You wake up rubbing your head. There's an ugly, tender bump up there. The bats are gone. In fact, the whole cave is gone!

You're lying near the center of the clearing, staring back up at the mountain ridge. It's dark now. Your head aches. In the distance, you can barely make out the glow of your campfire.

Whatever happened, it's all over now. The tower is gone. You missed your opportunity to find out what the tower wanted, and why you were supposed to be here.

Hey, at least you got to go camping. But sorry to break it to you, this is

---

THE END

150

You stop dead at the top of the staircase. A four-legged, winged creature sits calmly in the center of the next chamber. Its body is that of a lion, but its head has human-like features. The creature's long tail sways lazily back and forth as it follows you with its eyes.

"A sphinx?" you ask incredulously.

"*Yes,*" says YON.

"You gotta be kidding me." It takes a moment for you to digest the unreality of your situation. "Next thing you'll tell me is it wants to ask me a riddle!"

"*It does,*" YON replies. "*But I would advise against it.*"

"And why is that?"

YON pauses. *"Because the sphinx is... tricky."*

There's an elaborate archway behind the sphinx. You realize you have to go through it. "Go ahead," you tell the sphinx. At this point you're overtired, and beyond caring about a good number of things. "Ask me your riddle."

The creature gazes back at you with piercing eyes. You detect the hint of a wry smile as a new voice echoes inside your head:

A man and his wife have 150 pieces of gold.
The man has 100 pieces more than his wife.
How much does his wife have?

"That's easy!" you laugh. "This isn't even a riddle, it's a math equation!"

If you think the answer is '25' you should *TURN TO PAGE 25*
If you think the answer is '50' you should *TURN TO PAGE 50*
If you think the answer is '150' you should probably think again, because you're already *on* page 150! (Duh!)

151

The path continues, and this time you actually manage to keep up with the girls. You're walking between them when you notice something coming from the opposite direction.

"Stay back!" you order, flinging your arms out protectively. A long, jade-green snake is winding its way up the path. It's heading straight for you.

"It's heading straight for us!" Una cries.

You reach down and sweep up a fallen tree branch. Hoping to frighten the snake away, you hold it menacingly out in front of you. But the snake doesn't stop. It's still coming. Even faster now, actually.

"Wait!" says Kara.

"Don't wait!" says Una. "It's going to strike!"

Do you swing at the snake? If so, *TURN TO PAGE 34*

Or do you listen to Kara? If you hesitate, *GO TO PAGE 82*

152

Haltingly you reach out and touch the mirror. Rather than strike the glass, your hand actually goes *through* it. Ripples form. They bounce outward in a Doppler effect, and when they reach the mirror's edge the entire surface becomes fluid.

The other Tyler smiles at you. Leaning forward, he steps through!

"Hello!"

Your mind is blown. Your body is locked up. "Are... are you..." Your mouth goes dry. You can't even think.

"Go on," the other you laughs. "Say it."

"Are you *me?*"

The Tyler from the mirror smiles broadly, which is totally weird, because it's *your* smile. "No," he says finally. "Not exactly."

"Then... then what?"

"Hang on a second," your mirror-twin tells you. "Gotta do something first."

The other Tyler strides past you to center of the room. He picks up the broken diamond and swaps it out for the flawless one. Almost immediately the room lights up again. The new diamond glows brightly, only this time the beams of light seem a lot more focused. You watch as they're concentrated into thousands of tiny pinpricks of light that beam themselves around the chamber.

"Ah, there we go."

Beacons of warm light strike the dozen or so other mirrors positioned throughout the room. These also begin to glow. The other you looks on in excitement as the mirrors shimmer and waver. Their surfaces also turn to liquid...

... and a brand new Tyler steps out of each one of them!

"Thanks!" says one of you.

"Great job!" says another.

You stand there holding your head with both hands, fingers tangled frantically in your hair. Half the Tylers in the room look at you and chuckle.

"But... but..."

"Calm down there buddy," says the first Tyler. You flinch as he lays a reassuring hand on your shoulder. "This isn't nearly as complicated as you might think it is..."

"You wanna bet?" laughs one of your mirror-twins. His joke sparks even more laughter from among the other Tylers.

"Alright, alright," says the Tyler standing beside you. "Everyone settle down. We owe him an explanation, and it's going to be hard to give it if you're all talking at once."

"We owe him a lot more than that," says another twin.

153

It's all very surreal. Between the light, the mirrors, and the dozen or more copies of yourself – not to mention the exertion of having climbed all the way to the top of the tower – you're about ready to throw in the towel.

"Here," the original mirror-Tyler urges. He's offering you something. You look down and realize it's your canteen – the one you left back at your campsite.

You uncap it and take a drink. "Uh, thanks," you say. You notice half the Tylers around you are wearing your backpack. Half aren't.

"No worries."

You close your eyes for a moment, thinking it will make things less weird. But hearing your voice come out of a bunch of other people as they talk excitedly amongst each other is even more bizarre.

"So what happened?" you ask at last. "How... how is any of this possible?"

The Tyler beside you scratches behind his ear. You recognize it, of course, as *your* habit.

"Why don't you tell us what *you* think?" he suggests.

You search your thoughts. Your memories. Your gut instincts.

"Well..." you say, resisting the sudden urge to scratch behind your ear. "I– I'm pretty sure I've been here before."

Half the Tylers in the room roll their eyes. "You can say that again!" one of them cries out.

"I– I'm pretty sure I've been here before," mimics one of the other Tylers, trying to be funny. The rest laugh.

"Shhh!" says the Tyler who handed you the canteen. "Be quiet, let him think!" He waves off the others before turning back to you. "Never mind them. Keep going."

The room falls silent. You feel put on the spot. Thankfully however, things seem to be coming back to you in bits and pieces.

"The tower was broken," you say.

The Tyler standing next to you nods.

"That's why it kept blinking."

"Well, it was always meant to blink," the other you concedes. "It was designed for that type of travel." He points around the room. Every square inch of available wall space is still filled with glowing white star maps. "But it wasn't designed to blink so often."

"Or so completely at random," offers another Tyler.

"And that's all because the diamond was flawed," you continue. You point to the displaced gem in your twin's hand. "Somehow it got cracked."

154

Every person in the room spins at once. They all turn to look at one particular Tyler who stands near the rear of the group. He turns bright red.

"Yeah... the focus jewel definitely got cracked," your twin says sardonically.

Your mind is numb. Your whole body aches. You take another swig from the canteen before continuing.

"So..." You pause, searching for an answer. "So I was brought here to fix it?"

Your mirror-twins are all looking at you patiently. Waiting.

"Ah, the letters!" you cry suddenly. Reaching into your pocket, you pull out the piece of odd vellum paper. You hold it up and shake it. "I kept getting these letters!"

The Tyler next to you smirks.

"Yeah, somebody kept sending me these letters... and... and..."

"*Somebody?*" asks the other Tyler.

Then it hits you. You bolt upright like an electric shock, your face painted with realization! That's when you notice everyone in the room is smiling at you again. You can't help but feel foolish.

"It was me, wasn't it?" you ask sheepishly. "I sent *myself* the letters."

"Bingo."

You stare down at the piece of paper for a long time. Believe it or not, your own handwriting stares right back at you.

"How the heck did I never notice this!" you exclaim, shaking your head. "It's been right here! Right in front of me, the whole time!"

One of the other Tylers steps forward. "Don't beat yourself up," he smiles, "you had no reason in the world to suspect it." He waves an arm at the others. "None of us noticed it either. Not even when it was our turn."

"Your turn?"

The others nod in unison, like bobbleheads. All of a sudden you feel spooked.

"How?" you ask. "I mean, if I'm you... or rather, you're me..." you turn to face the nearest Tyler. "Are you *me* from a different period in my life?" The question seems ludicrous. You can't believe you're even asking it. "Me from six months ago? Me from six *minutes* ago?" You point at the symbols glowing along the walls. "Does the tower go back and forth in time?"

"Yes," says a Tyler.

"No," says another.

"Sort of," answer a few more of them. They all laugh again.

155

One more time you feel your own hand on your shoulder, which you've already decided is the strangest thing in the world. "The tower doesn't just teleport," the Tyler beside you explains. "It *traverses.*"

"What he means," says another one of you, "is that this place transcends both time *and* space. It's certainly not a time machine. It's a vehicle for visiting other... places."

"Mirror universes," the nearest you explains.

"More like multiverses," corrects the second one. "Copies of this place that exist *between.*"

You rub your eyes. "Between? What do you mean, between?"

"You're losing him!" warns another Tyler.

"Shhh!" the first one admonishes again. "Listen, think of it this way. You've been here before. Lots of times. But you've never really been *here* before." He stares back at you. "Got it?"

Slowly you give half a nod. Probably because you only half understand.

"The tower also travels to other places entirely," a Tyler says. "Other *worlds.*"

Your gaze goes back to the star maps. There are dozens of them. You consider yourself an amateur astronomer, but at a glimpse you can see thousands of stars and constellations you've never seen before.

"That's how YON got here," you say. "The tower picked him up from his home world. Just like it picked up a lot of other people. And things."

For once the other Tylers say nothing. But there's affirmation in their gaze.

"So... how did it all get started?" you ask. "What brought me – I mean us – to the tower in the first place?"

Your mirror-twin looks back at you with approval. Proudly he turns to face the others. "Ah, see? Now he's asking the *real* questions."

Just then, the diamond at the center of the chamber pulses. The star maps change! Everything is different; a whole new set of light-beams illuminate the walls in all new configurations.

"We don't have much time," the Tyler beside you warns. "The tower isn't long for this place."

You're suddenly concerned. "I thought it was done blinking?"

"Oh, it'll never be done blinking," the other Tyler replies. "But now it can be controlled. It can also be anchored, if need be." He looks over your shoulder. "Best of all, it can be used to put everybody back where they belong."

A cheer goes up in the room – a whole bunch of yous, all roaring together in delight. It's an eerie but satisfying chorus.

156

"So everyone goes home?" you ask.

"Yup!" the other Tyler says. "Una and Kara, YON and Kavalgyth... Finnegan too, if we can somehow drag him out of here. But yes. Everyone."

You look back at him skeptically. "Including me?"

The other Tylers laugh. "Especially you," one of them says.

As you watch, the Tyler with the broken diamond uses it to tap the nearest mirror. He does it three times in rapid succession, and the glass begins to glow.

"There's good news and there's better news," he tells you.

You raise an eyebrow. "Okay. Give me the good news."

"The good news is you're going home first." The surface of the mirror shimmers. It's now a bright, fuzzy orange. It looks exactly like every portal you've ever seen, in any sci-fi movie ever made.

"And the better news?"

"The better news is you don't have to walk." He smiles and gestures to the portal with a grand bow.

You step forward. Under normal circumstances you'd be hesitant to trust every molecule in your body to a glowing orange portal opened with a broken diamond. But these are far from normal circumstances.

"Wait!" one of the other Tylers calls from the back row. He pushes his way forward. "You forgot to tell him about the *best* news of all!"

The mirror-twin who opened the portal looks confused. "And what's that?"

Tyler from the back row reaches down and plucks the flawed diamond from his twin-brother's palm. Turning to you, he places it in your hand. "He's rich."

This time there are gasps from all around. The Tyler who opened the portal looks at you and shrugs. "Sure, why not? I suppose he is!"

Your heart just about stops. The jewel you're holding is tremendous. Even flawed, you know you'll never want for anything. Ever. Again.

"Goodbye brother!" back row Tyler calls out. You decide on the spot he's the best Tyler *ever.* "Oh, and hey..."

"What?"

He winks. "Don't do anything *I* wouldn't do!"

The journey through the portal is instantaneous. One second you're waving goodbye to a bunch of your mirror-selves, the next second you're standing in your campsite staring down at your feet.

Your fire is almost out. It's colder than ever. But the way the moonlight glints off your giant diamond? Well, that tends to warm you up a bit.

157

Suddenly the trees shake. The ground rumbles. There's a brief flash of light, and when you look back over your shoulder the tower is gone.

"Goodbye Tylers," you say to the wind. Then, stretching your aching legs, you go about the task of finding more firewood.

You braved the Tower of Never There!

Climbed every staircase! Conquered every level!

You also repaired the focus jewel, rescued the tower's trapped inhabitants, and made yourself rich beyond even your wildest dreams!

CONGRATULATIONS!
YOU HAVE REACHED THE ULTIMATE ENDING!

In recognition for taking up the gauntlet, let it be known to fellow adventurers that you are hereby granted the title of:

Sultan of the Shimmering Spire!

You may go here: **www.ultimateendingbooks.com/extras.php** and enter code:

HN71998

for tons of extras, and to print out your Ultimate Ending Book Seven certificate!

And for a special sneak peek of Ultimate Ending Book 8, *JUMP TO PAGE 181*

158

You lean your shoulder into the minotaur's night table. Pushing with every last ounce of strength, you manage to topple it.

It lands directly in front of the creature, tripping it!

With grunts of shock and anger, Kavalgyth the minotaur sprawls helplessly across the bedroom. His arms pinwheel frantically as he tries to regain his balance, but there's simply not enough room. The creature hurtles into the wall next to the fireplace with a resounding crash. And that's when Finny throws the blanket over him.

"Run!"

Before Kavalgyth can recover, you and Finnegan are sprinting full speed through another door. Corridor after corridor flies by. You go up ramps and staircases, climbing your way upward and through the tower. It's not long before the minotaur's screams of fury are fading behind you.

When you finally stop to catch your breath, you pull out the soapstone dragon. It's actually quite beautiful. You hand the figurine over to Finny.

"Nah," he tells you, waving his hand. "You keep it. Me and dragons... well, let's just say we don't get along."

You stare back at him in utter disbelief. Holding the dragon in one fist, you shake it at him furiously. "Well then why the heck did we just *steal* it?"

Finnegan smirks. "We didn't," he answers, wiping away sweat. "Like I said, a bet's a bet!"

That was some nice rolling back there! Slip the dragon figure into your pocket and *GO TO PAGE 138*

159

The rain hurts! It's searing your skin, burning your clothes... there's no way you can stay out in this!

Whipping around, you plunge back into the mist. If you can manage to stick to the path, maybe you can backtrack to the rope bridge. You concentrate on keeping the cobbles beneath your feet. At the very least, maybe you can outrun the storm...

You open one stinging eye. The mist parts just enough to reveal a large outcropping of rock. Desperately you dive beneath it, putting yourself out of harm's way. The rain still splatters down all around you, but thankfully, there's enough room to avoid contact with the burning liquid.

You huddle up and wait. You're cold and you're miserable. Most of your clothing has holes eaten through it, with red marks on the skin just beneath. You sit there wishing you still had your fire, but at least the rock ledge is keeping you dry.

Eventually the rain ends. The clouds part, and the mist clears. To your surprise, the sun is gone! In literally the span of a few seconds, it seems to go from day to night.

As you step out from beneath the rocky outcropping, the last of the day's light has escaped over the horizon. You've been riding out the storm for hours. You turn to face the tower...

And it's gone.

There's only the clearing, the stars, and the nighttime sounds of the wilderness. Some of which seem a little too close for comfort right now.

As you climb the slope in the direction of the camp, your only thoughts are of missed opportunity. What was the strange tower all about? What did it want, and why did it summon you here?

Sadly you'll never know. Because any last chance at answering those questions has reached

THE END

160

The ladder climb is brutal. It seems to go on forever, hundreds of identical rungs guiding you ever upward through a narrow chute.

Finally you reach the end. You pull yourself into a square stone chamber and immediately flop to the floor, gasping for air.

Suddenly there's movement. A humanoid figure strides into the room, made only of thousands of tiny lights. The lights glow silver and white, pulsating, shimmering, reflecting around the chamber in all directions.

You sit up. "Uh, hello?"

The figure stands there saying nothing. Then it points. Two orbs of smooth translucent glass are set into alcoves on either side of the room. One orb is red. The other is gold.

"Who are you?" you ask.

Once more the figure says nothing. Again it points – this time to the middle of the chamber. Standing in the dead center of the room is an ornate-looking, twisted metal stand.

It appears perfectly sized to hold one of the orbs.

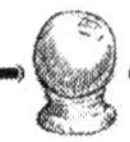

Yes, you're being forced to choose here.

If you place the RED orb on the stand, *HEAD TO PAGE 118*

To put the GOLD orb on the stand instead, *GO TO PAGE 78*

161

The dragon is close – too close. You're not going to let it get any closer.

Drawing forth the carved bone horn, you put it to your mouth and blow. It sounds long and low; a deep, resonating *BRRUUUMMME* sound that immediately causes the dragon's head to rear back!

In that split second the serpent is distracted, you scramble for cover... but there's no cover to be had. There's nothing around to even hide behind; not a rock, not a tree, not even a single shrub.

The dragon snarls back at you. It flaps its wings twice and moves in your direction.

Uh oh...

Got something *else* to try?

If you have the Lotus Blossom, try giving it to the dragon when you *HEAD TO PAGE 177*

If you have the Jeweled Pin, maybe that might be a better gift? Try it *OVER ON PAGE 81*

If you have the Snow Globe, you can shake it and hope for the best. *TURN TO PAGE 128*

Finally, when you were in the indoor garden, did you pet the Saspernink? If so, *GO TO PAGE 136*

If you obtained or accomplished none of these things, *TURN TO PAGE 68*

162

You reach out and grasp the card with the snake on it. As soon as you've plucked it from the table, the room fills with a loud hissing noise.

Finnegan groans. "Uh oh."

You spin around. Slithering up the staircase, a giant snake enters the room. Never mind giant... it's humongous! Its body is as big around as a garbage can, and its teeth are as long as your forearm. The serpent's head actually scrapes the ceiling as it towers over the both of you.

The snake is long and green. Jade green, in fact.

It flicks its tongue in and out as it heads in your direction...

"Better do something," Finny tells you. "Quick!"

Do you happen to know the snake's name? If so, use the chart below to add up all the letters in that word. When you have the total you can *GO TO THAT PAGE*

A = 1	F = 6	K = 11	P = 16	U = 21	Z = 26
B = 2	G = 7	L = 12	Q = 17	V = 22	Example:
C = 3	H = 8	M = 13	R = 18	W = 23	ANNA =
D = 4	I = 9	N = 14	S = 19	X = 24	1+14+14+1
E = 5	J = 10	O = 15	T = 20	Y = 25	= 30

If you don't know the snake's name, *TURN TO PAGE 132*

The purple smoke parts, and YON is standing over you. His hand (or what would pass for it, anyway) is right near your face. He takes special care not to touch you.

"*Wake up,*" he urges. "*We do not have time for this.*"

Something inside your head clicks, and you perk up. Vertigo threatens you again, but this time you rub your eyes and shake it off.

"Umm... thanks?" you offer. You're clearly still confused.

"*You can thank me by following quickly,*" YON tells you. "*This way.*"

Moving swiftly, YON leads you from the vision chamber. As you get out into open air, the fog lifts from your head as well. You're still moving slowly though, and have to run to catch up.

"What was that place?" you ask. But YON says nothing.

After a while, you find yourself at an intersection. Two corridors lead off in opposite directions. The light-being turns and stops. He seems to be waiting on you.

"Alright," you ask. "Which way?"

"*You must choose this path,*" YON tells you. "*I cannot.*"

There's not really any time to ask questions here.

If you take the LEFT hallway, *FLIP BACK TO PAGE 28*

If you head down the RIGHT corridor instead, *GO TO PAGE 113*

164

The pine door opens directly into a wide staircase. You furrow your brow at Finnegan.

"Why didn't we just take these stairs to begin with?" you ask.

He looks wounded. "What do you mean? We are!"

Sighing, you begin the climb. The stairs are made of pine also, and beautifully polished. You climb for what seems like forever, eventually stopping at a small landing to catch your breath. It's here that Finny pulls something from his pocket and begins gnawing on it.

"Want some?" He offers you what looks like a starfish covered in coconut.

"No thanks."

Finnegan shrugs and continues leading you upward. Just as you're about to ask for another rest, the two of you are spilled out into an empty room with a door on the opposite side. In the dead center, three large holes are spaced triangularly in the ceiling.

"The three-holed room," Finnegan says with a flourish.

You're still panting as you point upward. "So... what's with those?"

Finny follows your gaze to the ceiling. "Not sure, really," he tells you. "Always wanted to know though."

Hugging the wall, you skirt around the edge to the opposite door. There's no way you're walking beneath three strange holes. Not if you don't have to.

You're about to pull on the doorknob when Finnegan thrusts a slender wooden pole into your hand. You have no idea where he got it.

"C'mon," he tells you. "Pick one!"

If you poke hole number ONE, good luck and *FLIP BACK TO PAGE 45*

If you poke hole number TWO, hold your breath and *HEAD TO PAGE 174*

If you poke hole number THREE, suffer the consequences *OVER ON PAGE 140*

You can also hand the pole back to Finnegan and steadfastly refuse! If that's the case *GO TO PAGE 35*

165

The mist is rising. It swirls past your legs, your waist, your chest. It's almost at chin-height when you start to panic!

One last time you try the doorknob. In your frenzied efforts to get it unlocked, you accidentally turn it backwards...

... and it opens!

You fling yourself through, still holding your breath. YON follows and you nearly slam the door shut on him as he comes through.

With a long wheeze you empty your lungs. Then you breathe deeply, filling them with clean, delicious air!

"Thanks for nothing!" you tell your would-be friend. He sparkles briefly with a golden light, then nods.

"You knew the knob turned backward, didn't you?"

YON shrugs. He doesn't answer.

"Forget it," you tell him. "Stay here. I don't need you anymore."

A small staircase climbs out of the chamber you're in – the only exit. You take it without looking back.

YON follows anyway.

Keep calm and climb on *OVER ON PAGE 150*

166

The left-hand path meanders through another section of the colorful garden, this time through a fruit orchard. Kara and Una continue skipping ahead. You're so distracted by the beauty of everything around you, it's hard to keep up.

It's not long before you bump into them. The bough of a great tree crosses over the path above you. The sisters stand frozen, staring at it.

"What?"

167

The sound soon draws your attention. A large hornet's nest dangles from the branch, directly overhead. Strange green insects swirl around it in an angry buzz.

"Better go around," Una points. Already a small side path has been worn into the grass to avoid the nest.

"Wait," Kara says. "What's that?"

You follow her gaze. Something white and delicate has been woven into the nest. It looks beautiful, perhaps valuable.

"Should I get that?" you ask.

"No," Una declares immediately.

"Yes!" Kara cries, clapping her hands.

You're torn. On one hand, the thing in the nest looks like it could be important. But at the same time, there sure are a lot of hornets.

Una sighs. "If you're going near that nest – which I highly advise against – you should at least use a repellent." She reaches into one of her many pockets and pulls forth a small sprig of green leaves. "This is mint," she tells you. "Hornets hate it."

"Nonsense," Kara butts in. She steps off the path and plucks a succulent peach from a nearby tree. "This works better," she says, breaking off a few of the leaves and handing them to you.

You're left holding mint leaves in one hand and peach leaves in the other. Una is shaking her head. Kara is casually munching on the juiciest peach in the universe.

Do you rub the mint leaves on your skin before going near the hornet's nest? If so, *HEAD TO PAGE 114*

Or do you take Kara's advice and use the peach leaves instead? If that's your move, *FLIP BACK TO PAGE 21*

Of course, you can bypass the nest entirely. Forget the hornets and *GO TO PAGE 151*

168

The soldier keeps coming. You search your pockets... but you've got nothing!

"YON!" you cry. "Help!"

You scan the darkness, but there's no sign of your glowing friend. The soldier swings again. You duck under it. He thrusts the shield at you, but you dodge that too.

In a last ditch effort you look for the exit. Maybe the archway is still there. Maybe you can backtrack...

CLANG!

You wake up in the center of the domed chamber, between the four naked pedestals. Everything hurts. Your body, your spirit... and especially your head. Gingerly you touch the back of your skull, already knowing there's going to be a shield-sized lump there.

"Hello?"

Your voice echoes strangely through the empty chamber. Moving stiffly, you make your way over to one of the high-flung windows and peer outside...

Dawn.

Oh no.

The light in the sky is oddly different. The landscape, even stranger. Tall, twisted trees rise out of a thick mist, stretching high into a bright orange sky. It looks like the cover of some old, heavy metal album.

The tower blinked, you realize. *I'm somewhere else...*

Head in your hands, you slump to the floor in defeat. You got far. Really, really far! Almost all the way, actually. But alas, still not far enough.

Your adventure has reached

THE END

169

"Elevator?" you gasp. "There's really an *elevator?*"

"Sure."

"Wouldn't that be faster?"

"Definitely!"

"Well alright then," you say. "Let's take that."

"Great!" says Finnegan. "Follow me!"

You walk the hall for a long time, passing door after door. It's like being in a funhouse. You wonder if any of these doors could even be real.

"Finnegan," you ask, "how long have you been here?"

"Less than some," he replies. "Longer than most."

"Sorry," you say reflexively. "I guess you want to go home too."

Finnegan laughs. "Actually no. All my life, I've never really fit in anywhere. I like this place. It's kooky... like me!" At long last, the hallway ends. "Ah, here we are."

Sure enough, a pair of elevator doors is recessed into the wall. Finny mashes the button with one thick finger and starts tapping his foot.

"Besides," he adds, "this place isn't *all* bad." He looks you over. "If you stick around long enough, you'll see."

"Yeah, uh," you hold your hands up, "no offense Finny, but I'd rather be–"

There's a loud ding. The elevator doors open. Behind them you find...

A simple wooden staircase.

"Ah dang!" Finnegan declares. "I guess the elevator isn't in today. That happens."

"But... but..."

He pats you consolingly. "Sorry bud. We're gonna have to take the stairs."

"How could–"

"Hey, at least it goes up!" Finnegan says. "Some days it goes sideways."

Before you can even ask him what that means, Finnegan is bounding up the staircase.

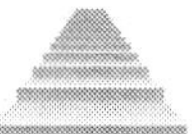

In for an elevator, in for a staircase!

Might as well follow *OVER ON PAGE 116*

170

Staircase after staircase, you and YON work your way through the top levels of the tower. After a while, the constant climbing begins taking its toll. You stop.

"YON," you gasp raggedly, "don't you ever get tired?"

"*No.*"

"Why not?"

"*Because I am not like you. I am a being of light and energy.*"

You glance down at your shirt. It's so damp with sweat, it's an entirely different color now. "That sounds pretty convenient," you tell him. "I need to sit down though, just for a minute."

YON flashes brightly a few times but says nothing. Apparently he's okay with waiting.

"You don't belong in this tower any more than I do," you say. "So tell me, what are you doing here?"

The light-being says nothing. He doesn't move, doesn't blink, doesn't change in color or intensity. You're fairly sure he's going to ignore you completely, when all of a sudden:

"*I am in exile. Imprisoned within the tower by my own kind, for a crime I did not perpetrate.*"

Your expression goes sad. In your mind you try to imagine YON's people marching him to the tower, forcing him inside. Watching as it blinked away, taking him from home.

"YON, I–"

Then, all of a sudden, you *do* see. It's as if another mind takes over your own, wresting control of your thoughts, your senses, your very memories. In the span of an instant, you are shown YON'S world! You see visions of his people, their culture, their cities and architecture...

You blink. Now you're shown the circumstances surrounding his exile. YON actually *is* innocent. And yet even so, he doesn't protest. You see him nobly abide by the decision that locked him away, watch helplessly as his exile unfolds before you. All of this happens in your mind's eye, in the span of single heartbeat.

When you blink again, your brain is once more your own. YON stares facelessly back at you.

"YON... I'm so, so sorry."

"*I do not seek pity,*" he replies. "*You sought to understand, to be enlightened. And so I showed you.*"

171

With that, the light-being rises and begins climbing again. It's not long before you're lead into a grassy chamber, lit from above by a diffused yellow light. An hour ago, a place like this would've seemed bizarre and impossible. But not now.

"Which way?"

YON points. Two exits lead from the area, both blocked by metal gates. To the right a black iron gate is already open, its arms swung wide. To the left, a silver gate remains locked. Its keyhole plate depicts two ocean waves crashing together, and looks like this:

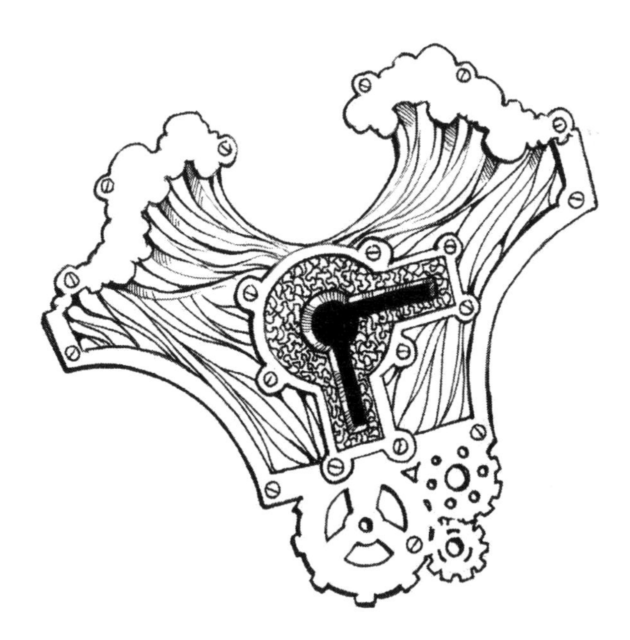

Do you have the key that fits into this lock? If so, what animal is crafted into the key's head? Use the chart below to add up all the letters in that word. When you have the total you can *GO TO THAT PAGE*

A = 1	F = 6	K = 11	P = 16	U = 21	Z = 26
B = 2	G = 7	L = 12	Q = 17	V = 22	Example:
C = 3	H = 8	M = 13	R = 18	W = 23	ANNA =
D = 4	I = 9	N = 14	S = 19	X = 24	1+14+14+1
E = 5	J = 10	O = 15	T = 20	Y = 25	= 30

If you don't have the key, that's okay. Just take the iron gate *ON PAGE 14*

172

You rush forward, knifing through the storm. You're half blind from the rain. Half deaf from the thunder. Trembling all over, you fall through the blue door...

Brightness. Light.

You glance around and find yourself back at your campsite! The sun is high in the sky now – it's the middle of the day. You're not sure how much time has passed, but the remnants of your campfire have gone utterly cold.

As you turn to look down at the clearing, you already know what you're going to see. The tower is gone. The entire area is now barren, flattened. As if something tremendous came along and just stomped a giant blank spot in the earth.

You start shivering uncontrollably, suddenly remembering you're still wet from the rain. Numbly you move to restart your fire, but it's only your body that goes through the motions. Your mind is somewhere else.

What was that place? Why was I there?

These are questions you'll ask yourself for the rest of your life. Unfortunately there won't be many answers. Your time in the tower has reached

---

THE END

173

The dancer whirls and twirls inexorably toward you. There's no avoiding her. Nowhere to run!

Reaching to your chest, you remove the exquisite jeweled pin Kara bestowed upon you. It flashes brightly, even in the dim light. With your eyes squeezed shut, you hold it out at arms length and offer it to the ballerina...

Abruptly the dancer winds down. She stops!

The girl plucks the piece of jewelry from your hand and pins it to her shoulder. Then she smiles at you, shimmers for a moment... and disappears!

The light in the chamber returns to normal. YON is standing beside you. Though he has no face to speak of, he looks pleased.

"*There.*"

The light-being points. In the center of the room, between the pedestals, a circular platform is slowly rising. Without hesitation you leap onto it. It travels smoothly upward, lifting you from the chamber.

When you look down to deliver a wave goodbye, YON is already gone.

You did it! Now *TURN TO PAGE 100*

174

Not knowing why, you take the pole from Finnegan and insert it into the second hole. You get beneath it for maximum leverage, then jab upward... hard.

"OWWW!"

A sharp yelp of pain comes from the opening in the ceiling! It's followed by cries and unintelligible shouting.

"Uhhh..."

The shouting grows louder.

"I think we should probably go," says Finnegan.

Yikes! Throw the pole to the floor and *HURRY OVER TO PAGE 66*

175

The card with the reaper on it looks very menacing. For that reason you decide it must be the safest choice.

"I pick this one," you say, lifting it from the table.

Finnegan automatically stiffens, every muscle in his body turning to stone. He squeezes his eyes shut and claps his hands over his ears.

"What?"

Apprehensively your friend opens one eye. He uses it to scan around the room.

"Finny it's okay, nothing happene–"

CLICK!

A hidden door unlatches itself along the left wall. It swings open slowly, revealing a narrow corridor choked with dust.

Finnegan relaxes as he lets out a long breath. "Whew! Good job!" He claps you on the shoulder. "That's *exactly* the card I would've picked, too!"

You grin skeptically. "Oh yeah?"

"Sure. Definitely."

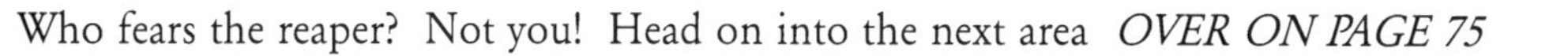

Who fears the reaper? Not you! Head on into the next area *OVER ON PAGE 75*

176

Scrambling to catch your balance, you pitch forward along the outside ledge. The chill night air bites your skin. The sky around you is a giant, reaching dome of stars.

At the very last second you catch yourself. You're going to be okay! But then you go to put your foot down... and realize you're out of ledge.

"*TYLER!*"

Finnegan's voice grows further and further away as you tumble into the darkness. As the side of the tower rushes by in a blur of stone, you have just enough time to realize this is

---

THE END

177

The dragon stretches to meet you. Its breath is fetid. Rivulets of slavering drool hang grotesquely from its maw.

Finally face to snout with you, its lips curl back in a vicious snarl...

On a whim, you think of the lotus flower Kara gave you in the indoor garden. You pull out. You hold it up.

The dragon blinks. Then, to your utter shock and surprise, the creature's expression softens!

Your arm trembles as you hold out the tiny flower. Ever so gently, the dragon takes it between its teeth. Its eyes bore into your own, and you see warmth there. Understanding.

Then, after a slow nod, the dragon leaps into the sky! It spirals away, high overhead, climbing and circling until you can't see it any longer.

The sky fades. The ground becomes stone again. You're back in the pedestal chamber! Only now, the part of the floor you're standing on is slowly rising. Up and up it goes, lifting you toward the dome.

Toward the very, very top...

Even the ugliest of beasts can appreciate great beauty! *TURN TO PAGE 100*

178

The angel swoops in for another pass... and you're out of options! You have nothing to offer her. Nothing with which to fend her off.

You duck again, but this time you're not so lucky. Two impossibly strong hands grab you, and you feel yourself being lifted from your feet! You no longer have any control. The room spins past you, flying by at a dizzying speed...

CRASH!

All of a sudden you're outside! Pieces of the shattered window rain down the side of the tower as the angel continues screaming into the sky. She carries you along with her, laughing the whole way. Circling ever upward...

Where's she taking you?

Will you ever get back down?

When it comes to those questions you're not really sure, although you *do* have a bird's eye view of the tower as it blinks away beneath you.

Wow, this is like the worst angel ever! And all because of her, this is

THE END

179

The next room takes your breath away, and that's because the floor of the chamber is made entirely of glass. It takes a full minute before you're willing to step out onto it. The chunky, semi-translucent material allows you to see straight down to what looks like a thousand-foot drop!

"Uh, do we *have* to go this way?" you ask hesitantly.

YON replies by gliding easily across the room. You follow him slowly, thinking extremely light thoughts and trying to step as gingerly as possible. You can see the floor is thick enough that it really makes no difference, but it makes you feel better all the same.

An archway exits the room on the opposite side. Inscribed above it is a riddle:

We are the same but not at all
A reflection of not me but you
Mirrors of each other's lives
Give or take a minute or two

The moment you finish reading the riddle, a deep, resonant voice calls out: *WHAT ARE WE?*

Think you know the answer? If so use the chart below to add up all the letters in that single word. When you have the total you can *TURN TO THAT PAGE*

A = 1	F = 6	K = 11	P = 16	U = 21	Z = 26
B = 2	G = 7	L = 12	Q = 17	V = 22	Example:
C = 3	H = 8	M = 13	R = 18	W= 23	ANNA =
D = 4	I = 9	N = 14	S = 19	X = 24	1+14+14+1
E = 5	J = 10	O = 15	T = 20	Y = 25	= 30

If you don't know the answer, that's okay. Head through the fancy arch and *GO TO PAGE 20*

180

You set the ballerina figure carefully on the ivory pedestal. As you do, everything around you changes!

The room dims. You can no longer see the walls, or the pillars, or anything around you. Even the pedestals are gone.

A figure appears, spinning through the shadows. It's a dancer. A woman. She moves with poise and dignity, twirling through her routine with such gracefulness that you're soon captivated by the sheer fluidity.

You can't see her face. Everything is in shadow. Yet the closer she gets, the faster she spins.

Soon you can no longer follow her movements. She spins faster and faster, until your eyes hurt. Your head hurts. The entire room is spinning!

The dancer accelerates even more. Her movements are impossibly quick. She's spinning right toward you!

You throw up your arms to stop her, but you know that won't be enough...

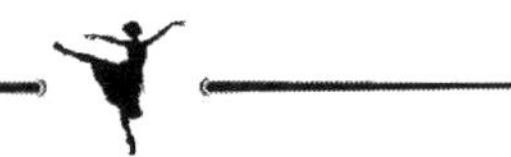

You'll need to act quickly here! What do you do?

If you have the Lotus Blossom you can offer it to her *OVER ON PAGE 121*

If you have the Jeweled Pin you can try that instead by *GOING TO PAGE 173*

If you have the Bone Horn maybe blowing it will stop her? *GO TO PAGE 67*

If you have the Snow Globe you can try shaking it and *TURN TO PAGE 24*

If you have none of these items, *TURN TO PAGE 137*

SNEAK PEEK

Welcome to the Kensington Airship!

You are BECKETT GRAFTON, a machinery tooling specialist at the London Airship Factory. For the past two years you and your brother BASTION have worked in the factory helping to build the Kensington Airship, the newest luxury airship that will make trans-Atlantic flights between London and New York. And it's finally finished! The airship is docked at the London Skyport and ready to make its maiden voyage.

You and Bastion saved up months of paychecks to purchase tickets. It would be the trip of a lifetime! You've never traveled across the Atlantic before. Unfortunately, due to high demand and excitement for the airship, tickets sold out immediately. You were unable to get a spot on the voyage!

But you're not the kind of person that would let that stop you. You've got a plan! And it involves a little bit of trickery.

It's early morning, and the fog is still thick over the London skyline. Carrying a backpack of clothes, you meet your brother at the factory where you work. He's already waiting when you show up.

"I feel goofy in this getup," Bastion says as you approach. He's wearing the navy jumpsuit of an airship engineer, with "Engine Specialist," stitched into a patch over the heart.

"Hey, it's only until we get aboard," you say. "You do want to get onto the Kensington, right?"

"Of course I do!" He frowns down at his uniform. "I just don't like these clothes. They're itchy!"

"We can change once we're on the airship."

You walk down the street, work boots echoing off the cobblestones. It's still early, and the roads are deserted. You feel a tingle of excitement for your plan. It's going to work. It has to!

182

You round a corner and the London Skyport appears in the distance, with a wall around the perimeter and a control tower off to the side. But what catches your eye is the object floating above it all.

The Kensington Airship!

Even though you've spent months helping construct the airship, it still takes your breath away. Long and torpedo-shaped, the helium balloon that provides its buoyancy makes up the majority of the airship's size. Connected below it are the rows of decks where the crew and passengers spend most of their time. It's built in the classic Victorian design, like a steampunk ship crossed with something out of a Doctor Seuss book, yet has all of the modern luxuries one would expect. It's like a cruise ship that floats!

Your excitement diminishes as you see the long line of people holding suitcases and waiting to board. The men wear suits and the women have on their finest dresses for the occasion. It's obvious that the Kensington is a luxury airship, meant for the rich and famous.

"Come on," you say, "the crew entrance is around the side."

Bastion follows you past the line of people. You don't mind the passengers watching you go by, but as you near the wall to the Skyport you see that the entrance is guarded by two London police officers. You feel their gaze as you go around the side.

There's a smaller line of workers waiting to get in at the crew entrance. It's similarly guarded, with a third police officer checking identification with an electronic scanner. Bastion stops at the corner. "Beckett, they're checking each person! How are we going to get in?"

"Relax. I've got it covered." You dig around in your uniform pocket and come out with two ID badges. Each has a photograph, the name and occupation, and a barcode at the bottom. You hand Bastion the one with his face on it.

"Engine Specialist," he reads. "Is this gunna work?"

"It'd better," you say. "I paid Jenny a lot of money for them! Come on, put it on and act natural. The guards are looking at us."

The police officers watch as you casually stroll to the back of the line. You wait as the line slowly moves forward. The police are really taking their time checking each worker, just to be safe. The Kensington's maiden voyage is a big deal! Everyone wants it to go smoothly.

You're almost to the front when the police officer checking identification suddenly says, "Hey! What are you doing here?"

She's staring right at you.

183

The officer, who has a sour face and a squinting stare, strides forward. You lick your lips and prepare for the worst. How did she know?

But just before she reaches you, she stops next to the man in front of you. "James! What are you doing trying to get on the Kensington?"

The man shakes his head. "I... uhh... don't know what you're talking about."

"Don't try this nonsense with me." The officer crosses her arms. "You aren't assigned to the Kensington. You were transferred last week, and you know it! So I ask again: what are you doing here?"

Instead of answering, the man whirls and tries to run away. He gets about twenty feet before the officer tackles him. "I'm sorry! I just wanted to be on the maiden voyage!" he cries while she handcuffs him. "It's not fair!"

"Well that's too bad," she says, pulling him to his feet. "You're on the second voyage, next week. You can wait until then."

"But..."

"No buts!" She drags him back over by the security entrance and dumps him in a chair. "Now you're going to sit here patiently while everyone else boards, and only when I'm on the ship and we're in the air will we let you free."

The man sighs and slumps his head.

The officer takes a deep breath and straightens her uniform, then turns to the first person in line. "Identification, please."

You and Bastion share a look.

The line creeps forward, and you're beginning to doubt whether or not your fake credentials will work. What happens if you and Bastion are discovered? The man sitting in the chair in handcuffs is proof that the police officer means business. You stare up at the luxury airship and wonder if all the risk is worth it.

Finally it's your turn. The police officer turns her gaze to you and Bastion and squints suspiciously. "I'm Officer Meredith Andrews. Identification, please."

184

You hand over your fake credentials. She examines the photograph, holds it up to compare to your face, then scans the barcode with her handheld device. The scanner beeps twice, and a green light flashes.

She stares at you a moment longer, and you give your most winning smile.

Finally she turns her eyes to Bastion and takes his ID. She blinks twice, and looks between the two of you. "Twins, eh? Beckett and Bastion?"

"Yes ma'am," you answer.

"Hmm." She examines Bastion's identification and looks back at you. "How do I know you're not Bastion and he isn't Beckett?"

"Well," you say, "I 'spose you don't. Good thing we both work on the Kensington, huh?"

"Mmm hmm." She purses her lips. "So, Bastion. You're an Engine Specialist?"

He swallows audibly. "Yeah. I mean, yes ma'am."

"Is that a fact? So if I were to ask you about the Kensington's four engines you'd be able to tell me all about them?"

You look sideways at your brother. A trickle of sweat rolls down his temple. It's obvious he's nervous, and could crack at any moment. "Well..." you begin.

Officer Andrews cuts you off with a finger. "I asked Bastion, not you."

Your heart begins to race. Although the two of you helped build the Kensington in the factory, you're certainly not engine experts. If she asks any details it will be obvious. If only the two of you had rehearsed your stories!

Bastion finally says, "Well, actually ma'am, the Kensington has six engines, not four. And yes, I can answer any questions you have."

185

Officer Andrews smirks. "Good catch, Bastion. No, that will be quite alright. The line's already too long as it is."

You give a sigh of relief as she takes Bastion's ID badge and scans it.

The scanner beeps once, and the red light flashes.

"What the..." Officer Andrews says. She frowns and scans his badge a second time.

Again, it beeps once and blinks red.

Uh oh.

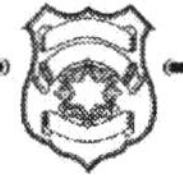

Uh oh is right! What next? Will *you* be able to figure out who committed...

SABOTAGE IN THE SUNDERED SKY

ABOUT THE AUTHORS

Danny McAleese started writing fantasy fiction during the golden age of Dungeons & Dragons, way back in the heady, adventure-filled days of the 1980's. His short stories, The Exit, and Momentum, made him the Grand Prize winner of Blizzard Entertainment's 2011 Global Fiction Writing contest.

He currently lives in NY, along with his wife, four children, three dogs, and a whole lot of chaos. www.dannymcaleese.com

David Kristoph lives in Virginia with his wonderful wife and two not-quite German Shepherds. He's a fantastic reader, great videogamer, good chess player, average cyclist, and mediocre runner. He's also a member of the Planetary Society, patron of StarTalk Radio, amateur astronomer and general space enthusiast. He writes mostly Science Fiction and Fantasy. www.DavidKristoph.com

THE TOWER OF NEVER THERE

WANT THIS BOOKMARK?

Review any one of our
Ultimate Ending books on Amazon
and we'll mail you a
glossy, full-color version!

Just send a screenshot
of your review to:
Bookmark@UltimateEndingBooks.com
and don't forget to include
your mailing address.

That's it!

(And thank you!)

NOTES

Printed in Great Britain
by Amazon